Spencer's Law

When Tazz Spencer first met Colena Hawthorn, she robbed him of both his clothes and horse! Little did he know that it was only the beginning of his relationship with this feisty young woman. When he earns a reputation by surviving a shoot-out with four hold-up men, he lands a job opening a bank in Penance, Colorado . . . with none other than Colena as the bank manager!

Now the action begins in this wild mining town! First Colena is kidnapped by a lustful mine baron who wants to sample her favours and then there's a robbery, a double-cross and finally murder. There was enough mayhem in Penance to keep three lawmen on their toes so Tazz faced an uphill task. Could he win Colena's heart – or even stay alive?

Spencer's Law

TERRELL L. BOWERS

A Black Horse Western

ROBERT HALE · LONDON

© Terrell L. Bowers 2003
First published in Great Britain 2003

ISBN 0 7090 7376 3

Robert Hale Limited
Clerkenwell House
Clerkenwell Green
London EC1R 0HT

Typeset by
Derek Doyle & Associates, Liverpool.
Printed and bound in Great Britain by
Antony Rowe Limited, Wiltshire

CHAPTER ONE

Tazz Spencer held the reins to his gruello mare while he knelt down to examine two sets of boot-prints and the tracks of a lone pack-mule. He was close, perhaps within a mile or two of the pair. Lifting his head, he tried to decide where Billy and Jo-Jo Akins were headed.

A creek wound through the hills, but logic dictated the Akins boys would try and rejoin their father and uncle. The whole family was about as worthless to society as fish-net umbrellas. They had been nothing but trouble since their arrival in the Cherry Creek area. A half-dozen complaints about theft and not paying their bills, three or four fights, and now the boys had beaten a trapper to death and stolen his furs. Tazz had managed to capture their horses, but the two had still managed to slip out of town. All four Akins were born for prison, and this time there would be no escape for at least two of them. Tazz would bring the pair before a judge or he'd bring in their heads!

He stood up, ready to mount, when he spied another set of fresh tracks coming in from another direction. The prints were from a lone horse, making its way down towards the bend in the creek. He had done some fishing along the Little Bear and recognized where the rider was headed. He swore under his breath, swung up into the saddle and put his heels to his mount.

He plunged the horse through the brush at break-neck speed. Billy and Jo-Jo were ruthless. They would as quickly kill to acquire a horse as they had to acquire the furs!

Tazz kept up the pace until he neared the brush and trees which lined the river. There he slowed his mount, searching for any sign of movement. It wouldn't do to have the Akins lay an ambush for him. Even as he was considering a safe way to edge closer to the water, he heard a woman's frantic voice.

'Help me!' the voice cried out. 'Please!'

Tazz threw caution to the wind. Straightening in the saddle, he sent his horse charging in the direction of the plea for help. He followed a marked path, winding through the trees, headed for the clearing. He raced between two large trees . . . .

There was a *swish* from a branch as it whipped about. Tazz was upright, unable to protect himself. His mouth opened with surprise.

But the branch caught him flush in the upper body and knocked him backwards, out of the saddle. His body slammed to the ground and the breath rushed from his lungs. He lay there dazed and momentarily blinded by the unexpected blow.

There was the sound of movement, then his hat was shoved down over his face. Before he could gather his wits, someone grabbed the gun from his holster.

'Lie still!' a woman's voice commanded. She

sounded as frantic as a scalded screech-owl. 'One move and I'll shoot you full of holes!'

Tazz twitched slightly and managed to swallow a gulp of air. He groaned from the hard landing, but remained motionless. He heard a set of feet pad softly over to his horse. From the sounds, he decided the gal was searching through his saddlebags. He had a little food, his shaving-kit and a box of ammunition. Nothing else.

'Keep that hat down over your eyes, mister,' she warned him a second time. 'You take one peek in my direction and I'll start shooting!'

'What's this all about?' he asked.

'Get on your feet,' the woman ordered. 'Strip off your shirt and pants.'

'Do what?'

'You heard me!' Her voice rose an octave. 'Remove your clothes!'

Tazz sat up and reached up to get hold of his hat.

'Don't!' the woman cried in alarm.

He heard the pistol cock and froze in mid-motion. Slowly, he lifted one hand to stabilize her apprehension.

'Only making sure I don't lose the louse-cage,' he explained. Then he adjusted the flat-crowned, black Stetson so it would stay fixed to his head, tipped low down to shield his eyes. Next, he rose stiffly up to a standing position.

'You are interfering with an officer of the law,' he told the woman carefully. 'I'm a deputy from Cherry Creek.'

'I don't care if you are President Ulysses S. Grant. You do as I say!'

'If you've had some trouble, I can . . .'

'Those contemptible thieves stole my horse – and everything else!' She curtly cut him off. 'If you had apprehended them sooner, I wouldn't be in this dilemma. In essence, this whole predicament is your fault.'

'Humm . . . sounds like a woman's logic to me.'

'Get started!' she snapped. 'I can just as easily strip your lifeless body!'

'You expect me to believe you'd kill me for my clothes?'

'First the shirt!' She ignored his question. 'I'm in no mood for tricks.' Uttering a sigh of resignation, he began with the buttons on his shirt. With a shrug he peeled it off and dropped it on the ground at his feet. Next, his hands went to his gun belt. He loosened it, allowed the holster to fall to the ground, then uncinched the belt holding up his trousers.

'Y – you do have something on?' The woman sounded apprehensive. 'I mean, *under* your trousers?'

He allowed a wry grin to play along his lips.

'And if I don't?'

'I am merely concerned for your modesty.' She excused the question. 'Keep going . . . and no tricks.'

Tazz loosened his trousers and let them drop. They piled about his ankles and it took him a moment to get them free from his boots. He backed up a step and stood patiently, wearing nothing but his hat, boots and under-drawers which only reached a few inches down his thighs.

'My summer hides,' he explained, aware she might be gawking at the cut-off long-handles. 'Too hot this time of year to wear a full set of drawers.' Adding with a smirk, 'I beg your pardon, if you're offended.'

'Step away,' she commanded.

'We can work this out,' Tazz offered, lifting his head slightly. It was not enough see the girl, but he was able to gauge her position.

'You raise your eyes another inch,' she warned him quickly, squeaking out the words, 'and I'll pull this trigger! I swear I will!'

Tazz gave a palms-outward gesture in compliance and once more lowered his head. The lady might be panicky, but she wasn't careless.

'Ma'am,' he tried to reason with her again, 'I have to catch and arrest those two men.'

'You can apprehend them tomorrow.'

'If we pool our resources, I'm sure we can work this out.'

'We have worked this out,' she stated firmly. 'I'm borrowing your clothes and your horse.'

'*Borrowing?*'

There was a slight hesitation. 'I'll leave them at the stable on Fremont Street,' she told him. 'You can claim them when you get back to town. I'll tell the livery man they are for Joe Smith.'

'There's an original handle.'

'Turn your back to me and move away,' she said.

He did so, rotating around and then pacing off a few feet. He listened while the woman quickly slipped into his shirt and trousers.

'What about my gun?' he asked. 'I told you, those are a couple of ornery critters. They would enjoy catching me waltzing about in nothing but my boots and unarmed.'

'I'll leave your pistol up the hill,' she offered. Then, as if it was an afterthought, 'I'll drop off a blanket for you, too.'

'I'm sure I'll make a fine-looking squaw.'

Her next words held a hint of humor. 'I hope no young bucks come along to molest you.'

'Yeah, me too.'

'If there were another way . . .'

'There are always alternatives to robbing a man and leaving him afoot, ma'am.'

'I need your hat too,' she said. 'Keep your back to me and hand it over.'

This time, Tazz did not oblige. Instead, he folded his arms in defiance.

'Did you hear me?'

'You've got my pants, my shirt, my gun and my horse,' he told her. 'If you want anything else, you can darn well shoot me to get it.'

'You would die for a stupid hat?'

'And I'm going to start counting,' he warned. 'If you are still here when I reach the number ten, I'm going to turn around and take a good look at you. I can tell you up front, I've a good memory for faces. No matter where you run, I'll find you.'

'Wait!' she cried, 'I'm no criminal! I don't have any choice about this.'

'Yes, you do,' he argued. 'We can work this out together.' When she didn't reply, Tazz started the ball rolling. 'One . . .' he began to count. 'Two . . .'

The woman didn't stick around to debate the issue further. She put his mare up the trail and kicked her into a run. By the time Tazz turned around, horse and rider were lost in the maze of underbrush and trees.

Tazz picked up his holster and started after the woman. He experienced a vulnerable sensation, being exposed and nearly naked, wearing only his hat, boots and abbreviated underwear. It provided him with an insight as to how the girl had felt.

He made the walk up the hill and was relieved to discover the girl had kept her word. He retrieved his gun and buckled it on. The blanket was not as important as the poncho which was rolled up inside. He slipped the oil slicker over his head and was adequately protected from the sun's rays. Clad in a poncho, boots and hat, he figured he would look pretty stupid to a passer-by. However, it was better than parading about in nothing but a pair of cut-off, red flannel underwear. Within moments, confined under the poncho, he was sweltering from the heat. Tazz reasoned: before the sun set he was going to have a keen empathy with a pork roast.

He tucked the blanket under his arm, slipped the canteen strap around his neck and began the long walk home. He guessed it to be about ten miles back to Denver. As the afternoon sun was fading to the west, it would be midnight or better by the time he entered town. Not altogether a bad time of night, considering his attire.

He maintained a steady pace, while considering the woman who had robbed him. No, not robbed – *borrowed* his clothes and horse. He had no doubt she would keep her word and leave his things at the stable. She had been a victim of circumstances herself. The Akin boys had taken her horse and clothing, so she had been forced to secure the same from Tazz. He wished she would have listened to reason. He could have provided her with his shirt or the poncho, and they could have shared the horse. Tazz would have taken time to return her to town, before continuing after the Akins boys.

Nevertheless, he didn't really blame her for the lack of trust. She had been robbed and was upset at being left with little to wear. On that note, he was forced to smile.

He had caught a partial glimpse of her, from her bare feet to about her knees. He discovered she was wearing pink, either silk or satin, bloomers. The material was damp enough for it to cling to what had appeared to be a pair of shapely legs.

He also thought back to when he had first regained his wind. Lying on the ground, he had detected a sweet fragrance – more than a soap, less than a perfume. He decided it might have been a scented shampoo, possibly a special liquid the girl used on her hair. He was going to remember that aroma for a long time.

Then there was the gal's voice, soft and pliant, like the whisper of an angel. She had threatened to shoot him, but he didn't actually believe she would have pulled the trigger. He had dealt with a good many tough men and rowdy women. He knew the difference between a bluff and someone frightened into acting irrational. He had a mind to discover the thief, more for personal satisfaction than to prosecute her for stealing his horse and clothes.

After making a steady climb to the crest of another hill, Tazz paused and took a drink from the canteen. The water was another reminder of the woman's regret and concern for his welfare. He hadn't ask for her to leave the canteen behind. Had she been only worried for herself, she would have ridden for town and not given him a second thought. Instead, she left him water, his gun, and even a blanket to conceal his lack of cloth-ing.

Danged if I ain't going to look that gal up, he vowed to himself. Any woman who frets that much about a man she is robbing, I want to meet in person!

It was early next morning when Tazz walked into the stable. He was stiff and sore from the long walk the previous day, but he was eager to get back in the saddle. He asked the stableman about his mare.

'You're Joe Smith?' the hostler asked.

'It's the name the horse and tack were left under.'

The man laughed. 'Yeah, I never quite seen anything like this before.' He went to a dust-covered table and picked up an envelope. 'One of the local runners around town brought in the horse. Left this note for you.'

Tazz took the envelope. 'Can you get the horse for me?'

'No problem,' he said. 'I was paid double the usual fare to stable the mare for the night. I'll throw on your saddle and gear and have her right out.'

'Thanks. I appreciate it.'

The man walked down to the row of stalls, while Tazz opened the envelope. He was surprised to find ten dollars in currency and a piece of paper. On the sheet were a few scribbled words of apology and an explana-tion that the money was for his inconvenience.

'You know the town runner who brought in the horse?' Tazz asked the hostler.

'Seen him around some,' he said, tossing on the horse blanket and saddle. 'I believe he sometimes does the cleaning chores at the Hawthorn bank.'

'You don't know his name?'

'Nope, but he's a youngster, possibly twelve or thirteen, skinny, an inch or two over five feet tall, with shaggy blond hair.'

'Thanks,' Tazz said. 'I can probably locate him.'

'So,' the man said, beginning to cinch up the saddle, 'you don't look like most Joe Smiths I get. They usually have the kind of face what's plastered on a wanted poster.'

'The person I loaned the horse to didn't know my name,' he explained.

'Uh-huh,' the hostler said. 'You lent out your horse and saddle to someone who didn't bother to get your name.' He paused to heft the saddlebags. 'Appear to have some clothes stuffed in your carry-all too. Mayhaps there is a little more to this here story.'

'I reckon it might seem that way,' Tazz admitted.

'And I'm guessin' you ain't going to shed no light on it for me?'

'It's a private matter.'

'Relate enough so's to whet my appetite, then tell me to go rope a goat.' The man grunted. 'Yeah, I know your sort.'

Tazz chuckled at his bewilderment. 'Thanks for tending to my horse.'

'Any time, *Joe*.'

Mounting up, Tazz decided to ride by the Hawthorn bank for a look-see. The Akins boys had a good lead, so

14

a few more minutes wouldn't make much difference. He was a hundred yards from the bank, when he spied Billy Akins! He was sitting his mount, pistol in hand, holding the reins of three more horses. Suddenly, the three other Akins men came out from the bank. Two were carrying sacks! It was a robbery!

'Hold it right there!' Tazz shouted, kicking his horse forward.

Billy spied Tazz and fired wildly. The three men on the ground were caught in the middle of the hold-up, not knowing whether to grab for their horse or start shooting.

Tazz returned fire at Billy – a lucky shot which struck him in the chest! He spilled out of the saddle, and the horses began jumping about, scrambling to get away from the gunfire.

The others were trapped on foot. Jo-Jo made a grab for a horse and missed. The other two turned their guns towards Tazz and started to blast away.

Tazz aimed and fired at Mont, the father of the two boys. He staggered back from the impact of his bullet. His brother hesitated to glance his direction. The lost instant was enough for Tazz to get off another shot, but the slug missed its mark, chipping wood near the door jam.

Jo-Jo was unable to catch up or gain control of the excited horse. He gave up the idea and began to shoot his gun as fast as he could pull the trigger.

Tazz felt a burn across his neck and there was a sudden, sharp pain in his left side. Even so, he kept his horse moving, bearing down on the two remaining men. Now, less than a hundred feet away, he took aim

15

and pulled the trigger. The older Akins man grabbed his chest and went down.

Jo-Jo panicked. He whirled about and started for the bank door. If he got inside, he would have hostages!

Tazz downed him with a bullet high in the leg. He buckled and crashed into the wall. Frantically, he spun around and extended his gun, desperate to get off a good shot. Tazz had fired five bullets. He had to make his last one count. Both he and Jo-Jo exchanged rounds at the same time.

Tazz was stunned by the bullet. It struck him a terrific blow to the stomach and he felt the wind rush from his lungs. He rocked forward in the saddle and pulled back on the reins. The jarring motion of the horse, as she came to a sudden stop, was more than he could handle. Tazz left the saddle and went over his horse's neck to land on his back in the middle of the street.

Dad-blame the luck! he thought, fighting through a haze of pain, I've been gut-shot!

There was the sound of shouting and the running of feet. A familiar face appeared moments later, as a man came to kneel over him. It was Katlen, another deputy. He quickly appointed a couple men to look after the Akins bunch, then he put his attention on Tazz.

'Good Lord Almighty, Spencer!' he exclaimed. 'You took all four of the Akins clan by yourself!'

'Not . . .' Tazz attempted to draw a breath, 'not without taking a couple hits.'

Katlen tore his shirt away and did a quick examination. He began to laugh and Tazz stared at him with a curious look.

'What the Sam Hill's so funny?' he asked.

'Your buckle!' Katlen said. 'The bullet is embedded in your belt buckle!'

'Lucky devil!' It was the hostler from the stable. 'It appears as if the bullet tore a path through the pommel on his saddle first. Must have slowed down the slug before it hit him.' His aged mug appeared over Katlen's shoulder. 'You're a lucky man, Joe Smith.'

'Lucky?' Katlen chuckled again with obvious relief. 'This here fella has an angel riding on his shoulder. No one is that lucky!'

'I'm still bleeding,' Tazz told him, recovering a little wind.

Katlen snorted. 'Ain't but a scrape along your ribs, and the nick on your neck ain't more'n a scratch neither. I've gotten worse injuries clipping my mother's roses!'

Another man arrived. It was a doctor Tazz had seen around town a time or two. After a quick assessment he said:

'Don't look too serious, but we'd better patch you up.'

Tazz tested his muscles. 'What about the Akins bunch?'

The doctor gave a negative shake of his head.

'Three are already gone and the fourth is fading fast. There's nothing to do for them. You're an exceptional shot, Deputy.'

Tazz still had a powerful ache in the pit of his stomach, but, with Katlen lending him a little support, he managed to get to his feet.

'I'll tend to the bodies and see to your horse,' Katlen told him.

'Come on, son,' the doctor encouraged, putting an arm around Tazz's shoulders to steady him. 'It isn't far, just across the street and down a couple doors.'

Tazz listened to the excited chatter from the crowd behind him. He put his left hand to his side and felt the wetness of his own blood. He pressed against the wound to slow the loss of blood and started his walk with the doctor.

'By all the saints!' he overheard the hostler proclaim, speaking to those spectators who were just arriving on the scene. 'I ain't never seen the like! Four men!' His voice was incredulous. 'He done gunned down all four of them by himself – and he was on a horse yet! No sir! Ain't no one ever seen the like of that before!'

A great number of people were gathered now. The hostler and Katlen were both relating the story to everyone who wanted to listen, repeating and embellishing every detail about the furious gun battle.

Tazz gave a last look over his shoulder at the four lifeless bodies. He had been forced to kill a time or two before, but never like this. Never four men at one time. He hated the churning from deep inside. Worse, he knew he would see the faces of the Akins men again. Every night, before he went to sleep, they would come to haunt him. He'd had no choice, but it didn't change the finality of the fight. By the might and fortune of his unerring marksmanship, he had taken their lives.

CHAPTER TWO

The picture in the newspaper displayed the four corpses, all laid out for coffins. There was a lengthy account about the gunfight in front of the bank. Knute Hawthorn was studying the article when his daughter entered his office. Colena Hawthorn pretended to be all business, carrying some documents for him to sign.

'The loan papers for Miller Cossins,' she explained, placing them on his desk. 'Everything is in order.'

'How are you holding up, my dear?' Knute asked, taking a hard look at her.

'I'm fine, Father.' She lifted her shoulders in a shrug. 'After all, I was lying on the floor with you during the shooting. I didn't see anything of the fight.'

'I know, daughter, but it was a terrible battle.'

'The last few customers have talked of nothing but the robbery attempt,' she replied. 'All I remember is the terrible agony of the last one – Jo-Jo, I believe was his name – lying on the porch. I've never had to listen to anyone die before.'

'It was tragic, but just. That brave deputy saved our livelihood. We had two payrolls on hand. It would have ruined us if those bandits had made good their escape.'

'Yes, we were very fortunate.'

Knute rubbed his chin thoughtfully. 'How is it you knew the one named Jo-Jo?'

A searing heat threatened to turn Colena's face red with embarrassment. She waved her hand in a futile gesture to dismiss the question.

'I met the two boys once before, during my ride. They frightened me some, but they didn't try and hurt me.'

'Well, thank God again for the deputy showing up when he did. If they had taken all of the bank's money . . .'

'Yes,' she agreed quickly. 'I'm thankful too.'

He shook his head in wonder. 'Funny thing about the aftermath, the hostler called the deputy Joe Smith, but that isn't his name at all.'

Colena straightened in shock. 'Joe Smith?'

Knute had returned to scanning the paper and failed to notice her sudden interest.

'That's what it says here. States the man had picked up his horse at the livery earlier in the morning under the name of Joe Smith. He supposedly was already in pursuit of the Akins bunch. He had a warrant for the arrest of the two boys.'

Colena suffered an instant concern. It was the man she had met – robbed of his clothes and horse!

'Is the deputy all right? Someone said he was shot during the fight.'

'A couple of flesh wounds,' Knute replied. 'He'll be up and around in no time.'

'I'm gratified to hear that.'

The anxiety which surfaced in her voice caused

Knute to give her a puzzled look.

'Do you know him?'

'He's an officer of the law, Father.' She evaded a direct answer, immediately shielding her eyes with lowered lids. 'He put his life at risk to stop those criminals and he saved our bank. I'm naturally concerned for his welfare.'

'I see.'

She didn't like the interested tone in his voice. 'I've never formally met any of the lawmen in Denver. The only dealings I've had are with the one or two who have an account here at the bank. I'm sure none of them was named Joe Smith.'

'But the man's name isn't Joe Smith.'

'Yes, I know. I was answering your question.'

'I didn't ask a question.'

'You didn't have to. I can read you like an open book.'

He didn't argue the fact. 'It's only that I worry about you, dear,' he told her seriously. 'Ever since your mother died, you haven't shown interest in anything or anyone, other than the bank. It isn't healthy for a lady your age.'

'Are you insinuating I'm an old maid?'

'You are ripe and beautiful, dear daughter. I've introduced to you eligible young men and had dozens of others ask about courting you, but you have never given any of them a second glance. What do you want in a man?'

'I'm not currently interested in romance, Father. I only want to prove I can do the job for which I was educated and trained.'

No sooner were the words out, than she realized it wasn't entirely the truth. The deputy had definitely affected her. Every time she closed her eyes, she pictured him in her mind. She could not forget his lithe build or the way his muscles rippled when he removed his shirt. Her recent dreams about the mysterious man with the hidden face had haunted her unmercifully.

'You look a little flushed.' Knute picked up on her reaction to the thoughts. 'Are you feeling all right?'

'I didn't get much sleep,' she told him truthfully. 'I kept reliving the hold-up.'

'Would you like to go home early?' he offered. 'Jory can watch the front desk.'

'Would you mind?' she asked, suddenly anxious to get away from the bank and everyone in it. 'I could really use a little time to myself.'

'Certainly, Colena. I'll see you at home.'

'Thank you, Father,' she said. Then she whirled about and left his office. She paused only long enough to pick up her bag, before going out of the bank. She did not hesitate a second, hurrying towards Fremont Street. She needed to speak to the hostler. If one of the Akins boys had been riding her rented horse, it would have been recovered. She had feared she would have to pay for the stolen animal, but now there was a good chance it had already been found.

As she walked up the street, she passed the doctor's office. It caused her to wonder where the deputy was at. It was only proper and befitting she face the man in person. She could apologize properly for her behavior at the river. Somehow, she knew he would accept the explanation without reproach.

No! I can't face him. I can't!

She hated feeling cheap and ashamed for humiliating the deputy. He had come to her rescue the first time, when she had taken his clothes and horse. The second time, he had saved their bank from possible financial ruin. Add to that, he had probably saved her from having to pay for the rental horse. Darned if she didn't owe that man a bundle!

It had been two days since the shooting. Tazz was on the mend and surprised by his visitor. The town banker had sought him out, visited for a bit and made him an offer.

'You don't know anything about me,' Tazz responded. 'We ain't been talking for more than a few minutes.'

'I consider myself a good judge of men,' the man replied. 'Plus, I've known your friend, Mr Katlen, for several years. He has vouched for your character.'

'Even so, I can't believe you want to hire me to work at one of your banks.'

'I need a man like you, son,' Knute told him. 'You risked your life to uphold the law. Your actions saved my bank from possible bankruptcy.'

'I was only doing my job.'

'Yes, yes, I know all that.' Knute's expression was eager. 'But I believe you are destined for better things. I'd like for you to come to work for me.'

'Doing what? Being a teller or something?'

'How does the title of Vice-President sound?'

'Me? Vice-president of a bank?'

'That's right, my boy,' Knute said cheerfully. 'I think

you are just the man I'm looking for.'

Tazz wondered if the banker's bacon had slipped off his plate. Who hired a gunman off of the street to help manage a bank? He studied the old boy for a reaction and suggested:

'Maybe I can't read or write?'

'I'm sure you can.'

'I don't even have an account at your bank,' Tazz said. 'I've never had enough money at one time to worry about where to keep it.'

'That's not important.'

'How about the fact I know nothing about keeping books or managing other people's money?' he wanted to know. 'That ought to be important.'

'The job I'm offering you is more social than cleri-cal,' Knute allowed. 'You would be a spokesman for the bank, a man to greet new customers or address their concerns. The paperwork, managing the money and other menial duties would be handled by the other employees.'

'Then you only want me as a figurehead of sorts?'

'Let's not trivialize the duties, Mr Spencer. You would be expected to encourage new accounts, handle secu-rity, and tend to the concerns of any difficult customers or situations.' He displayed a meaningful smile. 'The job I'm offering is over at Penance.'

'Penance, Colorado,' Tazz mused. 'I begin to see the need for a figurehead – especially one who can use a gun.'

'I admit your heroics against the Akins has some-thing to do with my offering you the position. You have proved yourself fearless in the performance of your duties. That's something I could use, Mr Spencer. With a man like you around, people would feel they could safely invest their funds in our bank.'

'Because I'm good with a gun.'

'There is that aspect, but I believe you are also capable of handling tough customers and preventing potential problems which may arise. Plus, there is a need for adequate security in a wild town like Penance. I'm sure your professional talents would be a valuable asset to our business.'

'I don't know, Mr Hawthorn. I didn't kill them Akins boys to get myself a reputation as a bad man with a gun.'

'Certainly not, and I'm looking for character, not a reputation.'

'I don't intend to cash in on the death of four men. I'm not proud I had to kill those fellows.'

'I should hope not.' Knute was quick to agree. 'I don't expect you to have to put on any displays of shooting skill, but your reputed prowess with a gun would act as a deterrent to any would-be bandits or the like.' He then changed tactics. 'How much do you earn being a deputy?'

'Sixty dollars a month.'

'As vice-president of my bank, you would be paid one hundred dollars a month and a percentage of the profits. I have a son, David, running a bank for me over in the town of Colorado Springs. He earned six thousand dollars last year. His vice-president collected about half as much.'

'Those are some big wages.'

'The railroad lends to a big part of their business

over there. I happen to know the rail had been desig-
nated to reach Penance in the next year or two.'

'I don't know. Working in a bank sounds about as
strange as a pig with wings.'

'We could try it on a temporary basis,' Knute offered.
'Let's say a three-month trial. If you don't feel it's right
for you after that time, you can pick up your chips and
move on to a new game. If it works out, I have other
ideas in mind for future banks. Who knows? You might
end up running a bank for me one day.'

'And I might be the worst banker you ever hired.'

He laughed. 'That's why the trial basis, my boy. Each
of us can assess the other's ability. This is a great opportunity for you. I think you should give it some thought.'

'It don't take much thinking on my part. If you really
think I can do the job, I'd be right proud to sign on.'

'Good. I'm sure you won't regret the decision.'

'When would I start?'

'I'm scheduled to assume control of the existing
bank by the end of the month. If you accept the position, I would expect you to visit Penance a few days
before starting work. You can get the feel of the town,
look over the nearby mines and ranches, that sort of
thing. I'll allow you a month's pay as a bonus for join-
ing the team and to pay for your investigative fieldwork.
You can get settled and assume your bank duties when
my president arrives to take over. That would be the
first day of August.'

'It sounds like a great opportunity,' Tazz told him. 'I
still think you're swatting flies in the dark, hiring me
like this, but I appreciate it.'

'I believe you are exactly the man I need for the job,

son. My new manager has all the business smarts in the world, but there is no substitute for someone who knows how to deal with people.'

'OK, Mr Hawthorn. I'll turn in my resignation and pack my gear.'

'Fine, fine,' Knute said, smiling. 'I believe this will be a consummate arrangement for us both.' He stuck out his hand. 'Welcome to the company, son.'

Tazz made the handshake and felt his spirits lift. His future was suddenly bright. Here was a chance to earn a great living, use his head for a change, and no longer haul in drunks or break up bar fights. No more cold camps or sleeping on the ground at nights while tracking criminals. No sir, he was going to be a banker, a regular pillar of society.

Colena was still amazed that her father had agreed to let her manage the bank in Penance. It had taken a lot of argument, but he had finally caved in to her pleas. She was on her way, but the trip to Penance could be a harrowing affair.

The Denver and South Park Railroad went most of the way, and the plans for the completion of rail to the Cloud City – also known as Leadville – were under way. However, the only actual tracks beyond the end of the line were narrow-gauge tracks for the individual mining operations. Narrow-gauge rails were only spaced three feet apart, allowing for maneuvering around the steep, confined canyon walls or for going into the mines themselves. As such, a regular train could not travel on the more compressed tracks. Also, the builders and operators seldom took passengers into consideration. As it was not safe for a woman to travel by horseback alone, Colena was forced to go by way of stagecoach.

Even at the best times of year, riding a coach was like being locked into a barrel and shoved down the side of a mountain. The roads and trails were deeply rutted from when it rained, and steep and treacherous through the hills. On the flatlands, the hoofs of the horses and the wheels churned up a powdery dust that smothered the wagon in a cloud and made breathing air nearly impossible.

Colena undertook the hardship of travel with a grim determination. As far back as she could remember, David had been the apple of her father's eye. He was the prodigy son, the boy wonder, who could multiply and divide huge numbers in his head. He was helping as a bookkeeper at ten, counting money and balancing books at twelve. She had grown up in the shadow of her brother's genius for banking. Eventually, after years of concentrating on nothing but education and work, she had won a chance to compete. She vowed nothing would stop her from succeeding. She would make her father as proud of her as he was of David.

Her companions on this journey were a liquor salesman and an aging tinhorn gambler. They were respectful enough, except the drummer constantly spat tobacco-juice out the window and the gambler smoked an occasional foul-smelling cigar.

They changed horses near a place called Kenosha and continued on a trail which wound up through the mountain passes. A cool bank of clouds greeted their descent into the lower valleys, followed by a summer storm.

The window-covers were drawn in place to keep out the rain, but this made it darker inside the coach. At each clap of thunder, Colena cringed inwardly and cowered against the seat. They continued at a slow pace until the coach finally stopped altogether.

'Creek is running too high to cross,' the driver called back to them. 'We'll have to sit it out for a spell.'

Colena wondered what period of time was covered by a spell.

The downpour continued for an hour more. The gambler and the liquor-drummer played cards, but they didn't ask her to join them. It was just as well. Colena was not a good loser, and she hated games in which chance often dictated the winner. In an actual contest of wits with the two men, she figured she would have them both broke and stripped to their underwear in about five minutes flat.

The notion of reducing a man to his underwear was not the smartest of ideas. The episode of how she had robbed the deputy sprang to mind. She agonized over her reluctance to go meet the man face to face. He had risked his life for their bank and been shot during the gun battle. She had lacked the courage to locate him and express her thanks and apology in person. A hundred times, she had considered going to see the man. Why hadn't she done it? Was she afraid of him?

No. It was something more primeval, something deeply personal, intimately private. She could not deny feeling a certain physical attraction for the man, such as she had never experienced before. The clandestine,

inner cravings assailed her each night and left her rest-
lessly tossing and turning in bed. The phantasmal being
who came to haunt her dreams was faceless, his identity
constantly hidden in shadows or by his lowered hat. But
the voice was like silken wine, tempting, soothing,
intoxicating, the words nondescript, yet equally stimu-
lating and captivating. She could not begin to put a
name to her ailment or affliction, but it was highly
disturbing.

She cursed her weakness, because now her silly
apprehension had forever doomed her to a life where
the deputy would remain a specter of her dreams, a
faceless spirit who stirred her heart and upset her
aplomb. Had she faced him in person, he would have
no such power over her. She would have seen him for
the imperfect being he was. There would have been
obvious flaws and weaknesses; the infatuation would
have been over.

'Hang on back there!' the driver shouted, breaking
into her melancholy disposition. 'We're going to try
and cross.'

Try and cross? Colena lifted the window-cover and
looked out. It was gloomy and dark from the storm.
The rain was still coming down steadily. How could the
river be any easier to cross now than an hour ago?

The coach rocked and bounced until it hit the water.
Then the team lurched against the traces as the swirling
stream hit the underbelly of the coach. The driver
shouted a string of profanities at the animals and
cracked his whip. The raging current fought against the
coach, trying to sweep the stage along the surging
torrent of water.

They hit a deep hole and the three passengers were tossed from their seats. The driver bellowed vehemently and there came another crack of his whip.

Colena and both men ended up on the floor. She was crushed between the two men. Before any of them could right themselves, the staged pitched forward, they bounced again and were suddenly back on the trail. As they began to roll along, a gust of wind blew a wet sprinkle through the open window. The gambler quickly pulled the cover back into place and they all retook their seats.

'We're in for a hard ride,' he warned. 'The trail's nothing but mud from here on.'

Colena didn't realize what that meant at first. She soon learned the stage could not avoid the holes and craters which lined the road. With the slick terrain, the wheels followed the deep ruts and the passengers were tossed about until they were battered and beaten from head to foot. It took all of her energy to hold tight and absorb the pounding.

The stage rolled into Penance after midnight. When it finally stopped, the three passengers could only stare numbly at one another. Colena's arms ached from clinging tightly to the door and the back of the cushioned seat. Bracing her feet had caused the muscles in her legs to seize tightly and constricted her movements. When the driver opened the door, she made the descent on wooden legs.

'Quite a ride, huh?' the old whip asked, displaying a grin which revealed three or four missing front teeth. 'By gum! We got here in one piece! That's what you paid for.'

Colena's brain began to work, as she lowered her foot to the ground, where her shoe sank into a layer of cold mud. The slimy surface-water came well up her ankle. She was committed to the act of disembarking, so she had no choice but to follow the entrenched foot with her other one. Her skirt dragged the surface ooze, while the driver gallantly placed a hand under her elbow for support. She waded several feet until she reached the steps in front of a establishment with the name of WORTHINGTON FREIGHT on its false front. Once on the wooden porch, she stomped the mud from her shoes.

Glancing at the building she saw that it was dark, closed at that late hour.

'What about our luggage and finding our rooms?' she asked.

'Being Saturday night, everything but the saloons are closed tight by now,' the driver responded.

'Are we supposed to sleep in the street?'

'There are rooms available at a couple of the saloons,' he stated.

'I made arrangements to stay at Miss Taylor's boarding-house.'

'Sure 'nuff! I know Millie, I does. I'm sure she'd get out of bed for a proper lady like yourself, missy. It's right up the street,' he pointed off into the distance, 'past the row of gambling-houses – big two-story house with a whitewashed picket-fence. You'll see it. She leaves a garden lamp burning all night for the sake of her boarders.'

Colena stared through the drizzle of rain. 'I'll find it. Thank you.'

'I'll stow your things inside the office. You kin pick them up in the morning.'

'I know the guy at the Open Pit saloon,' the drummer informed the gambler. 'We can get a couple rooms there for a pretty cheap price.'

The other man bobbed his head affirmatively. 'Any place where I can lay down my sorry bones sounds good to me. I'm about done in.'

Colena waited until the driver unloaded the suitcases and bags. She had a small valise which held most of her personal items. The two trunks of clothes would have to remain at the office overnight. There was no walkway along either side of the street. Some businesses had an extended porch, while others had placed a few planks here and there for access. Colena determined it would be all she could manage to reach the boarding-house carrying a single, small bag.

The rain was more drizzle than downpour, but there was no shelter or overhang from the freight office or any other porch roof until the second saloon up the street. From the blaze of lights, the tinkle of a piano, loud voices and occasional obstreperous laughter, it appeared the storm had done little to slow business on a Saturday night.

Colena wore only a thin jacket over her bodice and heavy skirt. She had brought a light-weight parasol, but it was packed away in one of the trunks. Although protected by her hat, her hair was damp and disheveled from the drizzle, the rough ride and long hours in the coach. She might have removed her shoes in an attempt to save them from ruin, but they were the lace-up sort and were already caked with mud. Her first order of business was to simply get to someplace dry, where she could remove the muck from her feet and discard some of the dust from the long ride.

'The freight office ain't open for business on Sunday,' the driver told her. 'But someone will be around to fetch your things to the boarding-house.'

'Thank you, driver,' she said. 'I'll be fine.'

He put a single finger up to touch the brim of his sombrero-style hat, a show of courtesy probably reserved for very few people.

'Good night, ma'am.'

She nodded in return, took a deep breath, and plunged down from the porch and onto a wide plank. It sank until the water oozed an inch or two over the surface top and made the footing slippery and uncertain. The boarding-house appeared to be a mile away.

Colena slipped off the plank several times and ended up sloughing her way through the deep mire until she reached the next section of porch. The cold water penetrated and ran into her shoes. She felt it squish between her toes with each step.

Two men suddenly staggered out of the saloon and stopped on the porch, blocking Colena's path. She was forced to halt and wait for them to move out of the way.

'Wa'al, looky at what we found!' the one man said, ogling Colena. 'It's my dream woman! She's come to make my world complete!'

'Ain't no such thing,' the other man declared. 'I done saw her first!'

They moved as one, trapping her between them. The two smelled of sweat and hard liquor, both with leering eyes and slobbering over every word.

'Tell Boyle to take his'self on a hike, little lady,' the one offered. 'Me and you can have some fun together.'

'Peters,' the other man grunted, 'you ain't got what this lady needs. She's the sort what needs a real man.'

'Step aside and let me pass,' Colena said icily, displaying an uncertain bravado. 'I'm not one of your town harlots.'

'Hear that, Boyle?' Peters slurred the words. 'She ain't one of your kind a'tall.'

'Ain't your'n neither,' the other man retorted.

'Wa'al, guess there's only one thing to do then,' Peters offered with a grin.

Boyle laughed coarsely. 'Yeah, we'll just have to share!'

'I am a proper and genteel lady.' Colena scalded the two men with a harsh tone of voice. 'Remove yourselves from the pathway or I'll have you arrested.'

Peters frowned, his plug-ugly mug contorted into disbelief.

'By golly! She done *sounds* like a real lady, Boyle. I ain't never met no lady out walking at this hour afore.'

'You ain't telling me nuth'en,' Boyle replied in awe. Then, with a dog-serious look: 'How 'bout we two cavalier sorts escort her home?'

'I can manage by myself,' Colena said, controlling her patience.

'We got to insist,' Peters told her. 'Who knows what kind of ungentlemanly types you might run into.'

'I said to get out of my way!' Colena snapped off the words and swung the valise at the nearest man.

'Hey!' Peters shouted, ducking back from the attempt. 'We're being polite!'

'I don't require the escort of two inebriated oafs. Leave me alone!'

'Whatever happened to gratitude?' Boyle asked. 'We're being as respectful as two mice at a cat rally and the lady starts swinging at us with her big purse!'

'Yeah – and she calls us names! We ain't no *inebriates*, we's both American!'

'Get away from me!' Colena demanded. 'Move or I'm going to scream!'

'Wa'al, hell's bells, woman!' Peters growled. 'You ain't much of a lady. You try and hit us, you want us arrested, and now you threaten to start screaming for help. What the duce is wrong with you?'

Colena had eaten horrible food, drunk tepid water, choked down dust and been trapped with two unbathed men in a bumpy coach for sixteen hours. She was tired, aching, and soaked from the rain and mud. Her patience was not thin, it was non-existent.

'I said to remove yourselves from my path!' she hissed. And with a deliberate step forward, she stomped down on Boyle's foot!

'Yeow!' he bellowed.

Colena again used the valise like a club and swatted at Peters. The men were driven back before her attack, hands raised to protect themselves from her fury.

'What the devil is wrong with you, woman?' the man bellowed. 'Stop swinging that piece of luggage at us!'

'Leave me alone!' she cried. 'Get away from me!'

Abruptly, a third man arrived. He gave no verbal warning, but grabbed Peters by the collar, yanked him around and bodily threw him off the porch. Peters tried to catch his balance at the hitching post, but his body had too much momentum. He hit the cross-pole below his waist and was upended, going right over the hitch rack. He landed in the black mire on his back with a *splat*!

Boyle saw what had happened to his friend. He stopped fending off the girl's flying valise and took a swing at the fresh arrival.

Ducking the roundhouse punch, the new man caught hold of the front of Boyle's shirt, whirled about, and tossed him into the street. The strength of the throw propelled Boyle off the porch and his stubby legs couldn't keep up with the speed of his body. Boyle sprawled, face first, sliding along in the thick bog, right into Peters. The two of them remained there, tangled up together, both cursing the mud, the newcomer, the woman, and their cold and slimy predicament.

'Beg your pardon, ma'am.' The rescuer spoke to Colena. 'These two rowdies didn't mean you any harm. They're only feeling their oats from too much to drink.'

Colena gasped in shock and threw a hand up over her mouth. She knew that voice! It was the deputy!

CHAPTER THREE

Tazz smiled at the lady, curious at the way she backed away from him. She acted as if he intended her a bit of harm. 'It's OK, ma'am,' he tried to reassure her. 'Them fellows won't give you any more trouble.'

'I – I was in no danger, sir!' the woman replied in a stern and throaty tone of voice. 'You didn't have to interfere on my behalf. I had the situation under control.'

'I didn't mean to butt in,' he said politely. 'I thought—'

'Yes, yes,' she was abrupt and seemed frantic to get away from him. 'I know what you thought. Now, if you'll excuse me . . .'

But he caught hold of her wrist. 'It'll be a mite safer if I see you home.'

She glared at him with fire in her eyes. 'Unhand me, sir!'

Instead of obeying, he gave her another easy smile. 'Reckon you've about had enough of men grabbing and pawing at you, but I'm only offering a courtesy.'

'I told you, it won't be necessary.'

'I ain't giving you a choice, ma'am. You can't be out on the street alone . . . not at this late hour . . . and not on a Saturday night. It's not proper for a lady.'

The woman sighed in defeat and tilted her head towards the stage depot. 'I only arrived in town a few minutes ago. I'm on my way to Miss Taylor's boarding-house.'

Tazz chuckled at the news. 'Say! It's a small world, ain't it?'

Oddly enough, the color left the young lady's face. He wondered at the sudden alarm. 'I mean,' he clarified his statement, 'I'm staying there myself.'

She appeared to recover. 'Oh,' was the only word to escape her lips.

'I was in the process of calling it a night when I noticed you having some problem with the two regulators.'

'There was no basis to dispense such a dispropor-tionate violence,' she said.

'I didn't use none of that dis-portion-ate stuff,' he argued, not fully comprehending her words. 'I used plain language they would be sure to understand.'

'Of course you did,' she allowed, pausing to glance at the two men. They were up on their feet and had moved over to the watering trough to rinse off some of the mud from their hands and clothing.

'How about we get you out of this rain?' he suggested.

The lady was no longer under the shelter of an over-hang. It was raining harder again, a steady shower which saturated her clothing and had her traveling hat warped to her head like a Quaker's bonnet.

'You called those two regulators?' she asked.

'Harcore Worthington's men. They are supposed to be something like peace officers around town.' He laughed at the idea. 'Except I've noticed those two are worse than most of the miners they are supposed to ride herd on.'

'They are a charming pair.'

'I expect they're a little better behaved when they're sober.' He excused their actions with an off-hand gesture. 'Come along with me, ma'am. I wouldn't want you to encounter another drunk or ill-mannered gent.'

'Thank you, but I really don't require your protection.'

He didn't move. 'Like I done said, it ain't open for discussion.'

'Who appointed you paladin of Penance?' she snapped angrily. 'I told you, I am not in need of your assistance!'

He raised his brows in puzzlement. 'What's one of them there paladins?'

'Never mind! I only wish to be left alone!'

'I'm sure going to do that, just as soon as I get you home for the night.' He glanced upward, the action causing a trickle of water to spill from the brim of his hat. 'What do you say, ma'am? We're getting pretty wet standing here in the rain.'

She uttered a sigh of resignation. 'You're both exasperating and pig-headed, sir!'

'Yes, ma'am.' He didn't take offense, simply turned around and held out his arm in gentlemanly fashion. 'Shall we get moving?'

She ignored his offered arm. 'All right! If you insist

. . . anything to escape this frightful downpour!'

He made a reach to take the valise, but the girl shifted it from one hand to the other to prevent it. The lady struck him as being about as skittish as a freshly broken mustang. Tazz stepped over to assume the inside position and they started off together.

After a short way, the lady began to walk a little closer, especially when they progressed past the loud, foul-smelling saloons. By the time they reached the end of the wooden walk, she was cuddled near enough to rub shoulders with him.

'It's a real mess from this point on,' he warned her. 'No planks, only mud.'

'Don't concern yourself,' she said. 'My shoes are already ruined.'

'Still, it don't seem proper.'

'I'll be fine, sir. Let's get on with it!'

It wasn't right with Tazz.

'No, ma'am,' politely, 'I believe I'll lend a hand.' Before the lady realized what he had in mind, he bent down, slipped an arm under the back of her legs and swept her up into his arms!

'What do you think you're doing!' she cried, squirming at once to get free of his grasp. 'Put me down!'

'Hold still!' he commanded sharply. 'You want me to drop you on your duff?'

'I won't have you carrying me!' she squealed. 'I told you, my shoes are already covered with mud.'

'We might still save your dress, ma'am. I told you, there's no planks from here on, only an ocean of bog. I've been to and from a couple times, so I know where to step in order to avoid some of the worst spots.'

41

'You antediluvian primate!' she blasted him hotly. 'Why must men be so predisposed to continually assert their physical dominance?'

'Pardon me?' he asked, beginning to tread the slippery footing. 'What language is that you're speaking?'

'It's called English! I'm sure your mother taught you a few basic grunts!'

'Better than that,' he replied. 'I can cipher numbers and read too. Facts be known, I've done read a fair portion of the Good Book.'

'How impressive,' she said drily.

'Yep, and the Bible done uses a bunch of words what sometimes don't make much sense neither. Still, with all my learning, I got to admit, I don't recognize a good many of them there words you're spouting at me.'

'It must be boring,' she continued to dig her spurs into him, 'to only read Bible passages comprising of words with less than two syllables.'

Tazz began to lose patience. 'Blamed if you ain't about the most contrary critter I ever come across, lady. I'm only trying to help you get to the boarding-house in the best shape possible.'

'And I explained that I was perfectly able to traverse the quagmire without your assistance!'

At that moment, he slipped a bit and had to catch himself. A cry rose from the girl's lips and she automatically shifted the valise. It struck Tazz in the ribs and caused him to grimace from the immediate streak of pain.

He remained completely still for a few seconds, slightly doubled at the middle. After taking a couple deep breaths, he straightened up again.

'Sorry,' he grunted the words, 'I've a bit of a sore spot on my side. That there satchel of yours caught me right where it's most tender.'

Surprisingly, the girl ceased struggling. 'I – I'm sorry,' she murmured, appearing to be genuinely concerned. 'I didn't mean to hurt you.'

He recovered his strength and began to plod the uncertain ground once more. After a few steps, he spoke up again. 'Like I was telling you, over at the end of the walk, there's some powerful deep holes.'

She glanced down at the dark, sloppy trail. 'I don't perceive any abysmal craters.'

'It's deceiving, ma'am. It sure is.' He tipped his head to one side and gave her a half-smile. 'Fact is, on my way to the gaming-house, I happened to see a freight wagon and team start through one of these here puddles and it plumb sank right out of sight.'

'What?' she asked, a frown of disbelief on her face.

'Yep. I reckon man and horse alike would have drowned, if that there draft team hadn't been good swimmers.'

'I thought the men who told the biggest lies were from Texas,' she said.

'Don't know who you've been talking to,' he replied. 'We here in Colorado can hold our own against the best of them.'

As they proceeded, he asked her: 'You just here for the night?'

'No, I'll be staying a while.'

'Takes some getting used to,' he warned. 'Civilization ain't exactly caught up with Penance yet.'

'I concluded as much from the encounter with the

43

local regulators and your own overzealous, asserted gallantry.'

'Dang, but you sure talk pretty,' he praised, glancing down at her. 'You're one of them educated types, aren't you?'

'I know what you're thinking – education is wasted on a woman. According to you men, a woman is supposed to stay home, mend, sew, bake bread and have children!'

'Hold up the team there, lady!' he protested. 'You're about as touchy as a shave-tail mule.'

'And what, pray tell, is a shave-tail mule?'

He again showed her his easy grin. 'Mule skinners shave the tails of green, unbroken mules. It's so people know not to walk or approach one of them suddenly from behind. Saves getting kicked in places that are best left unkicked!'

'A mule – what a lovely comparison,' she said curtly.

He ignored her retort. 'So, tell me,' he wanted to know, 'do you have a formal type education? I mean more than going to one of the local town schools?'

'Yes. I attended college.'

'Well, that's really something,' he exclaimed. 'I haven't had the privilege of meeting many scholarly types – man or woman. I know there are a good number of colleges admitting females these days. Did you go back East or somewhere closer?'

'Vassar.'

'Yep, heard of that place too,' he told her with some pride. 'I remember it started up after the end of the war between the Union and Confederacy.'

'My father insisted I go to a school for women only.'

'Figured you might get on a side trail and not come back otherwise, huh?'

'Something like that.'

'Here we are.' He turned down a firmly packed walkway, which led to a two-story house. A single light illuminated the yard. He continued up to the porch, where he stopped to place her gently down onto her feet.

She waited while he opened the door and held it for her.

Perched on the threshold, she peeked inside hesitantly. 'How am I supposed to know which room? I wired ahead to confirm my reservation, but . . .'

'Not a problem there,' he assured her. 'Mrs Taylor keeps a record at her desk. Each room has a letter from the alphabet painted above the door. We can have a look-see and find out where she intended to put you. We'll get you squared away for the night.'

'Are you certain such an intrusion is permissible?'

'Desk is right inside the door,' he said, motioning to one side of the room. 'If you want to take a look, I'll hold the door open for light.'

'Just a minute,' she said, placing the valise on the wooden platform and moving over to use the edge of the porch to scrape some of the mud from her shoes. 'Hate to leave any more mud than necessary.' She explained the obvious.

'Miss Taylor is a hound about keeping things clean,' he informed her. 'If you'd like, I could rinse off your shoes in one of the puddles.'

'No,' she answered, 'this will have to do.'

He continued to stand in the doorway as she

retrieved her single piece of luggage and passed by him. She might have been tired from a long journey by stage, but as she walked away from him, her hips had an enchanting feminine sway from side to side.

She reached the desk and, using the dim light, examined the book.

'It indicates I'm to stay in room "B",' she whispered.

'Bottom floor,' he replied back, also in a hushed voice. He pointed to a hallway and several doors beyond a stairway. 'A, B and C downstairs. D, E and F upstairs. I'm in D, should you ever need to know.'

'Thank you.'

'If you want, I'll fire the lamp in your room.'

'I'm sure I can manage on my own.'

'Should you get cold, there's extra blankets in the hall closet,' he advised.

'Thank you,' she said quietly, then walked over to her room. She paused at the door and looked back at him. 'You've been very much a gentleman.'

'Pleasure was all mine,' he replied. 'Mayhaps I'll see you at the breakfast table. Mrs Taylor serves two fine meals a day – both at six-thirty sharp. If you ain't there by seven, you're out of luck.'

'I'll remember.'

He reached up and tipped his hat respectfully. The action allowed a lock of unruly hair to dangle down onto his forehead.

'I'll say good night and let you get settled.'

'Thank you again for seeing me home safely.'

He flashed a wide grin. 'Yes, ma'am. It was my pleasure.'

*

Tazz was out of bed, shaved and dressed in time for breakfast. However, as it was Sunday, Millie only set out a kettle of grits and some hard bread. After Sunday meetings, there was always a picnic of sorts. Therefore, the boarders were on their own for supper.

When time came for the meeting, Tazz located a place at the rear of the room, where he could sit on a stool and lean his shoulders back against the thick, pine-slab wall. He joined in on a song or two, the ones to which he knew some of the words, and basically got a feel for the people of Penance. They seemed to be good folks.

The young lady whom he had met and escorted home the previous night arrived with Millie. She wore a full skirt, minus the bulky and cumbersome crinoline. Such attire was not suitable for the mining country or crowded quarters. The material of her outfit appeared durable and was a dark blue, matching the Eton jacket, which she wore over a plain white blouse. She did have several petticoats beneath the skirt, and a modest French-fashion hat was atop her neatly styled, butter-nut-colored hair.

There was something familiar about her, but he wasn't quite sure why. She had arrived by stage, but she could have departed from any point east of Penance. He knew their trails had crossed at one time, but darned if he could put a time and place to it. He hadn't met very many beautiful women, and this lady, she was – what was a good description... exquisite? Yeah, there was the right word. She shone like a polished jewel, full of fire and light. It didn't stand to reason he could have met some-one like her and not remember when or where.

The man on the pulpit was Phil Token, the editor of the town newsletter, a signmaker and a fair fill-in speaker for a parson. He was dressed in a store-bought suit and had neatly groomed hair and a black mustache about as narrow as a stalk of straw. He read from the Good Book and led the congregation through a prayer and several songs of praise to the Lord. Finally, he paused and looked out over the gathering.

'We have a new lady in our midst,' he began, looking at the girl next to Millie. 'Madam, would you please stand, so everyone can get a look at you?'

A bit of color came into the young woman's cheeks, but she rose up and displayed a smile of greeting to all those around her.

'Everyone, please join me in offering a warm welcome to Miss Colena Hawthorn. She has come all the way from Denver and is going to assume control of the bank.'

Tazz gaped in amazement. *By hanna! That's who she is!* He remembered the slight fragrance in the air at their first meeting. He had noticed a hint of the same aroma when he carried her along the muddy path. She had not sounded the same, but she was probably hoarse or tired from the long journey. Still, there could be no doubt, she was the bandit with the pink-satin bloomers!

With the mystery woman now clear in his mind, he began to worry about his new job. Colena was here to take over the bank. She was going to be his boss! He had gotten a taste of the girl's fiery temperament the previous night. She was quick to rile and didn't seem a woman who wanted to be indebted to anyone. As soon as she learned he was the deputy from Cherry Creek, she would know it had been his horse and clothes she had stolen! Things were going to be right awkward between them for a spell.

'Miss Hawthorn is staying at Millie's boarding-house,' Phil continued his introduction. 'Her father manages a bank in Denver and owns three banks in all. We want to wish her the best of luck and a warm welcome to Penance.'

Several people applauded and others spoke from nearby to convey their best wishes. The lady rotated about to make eye contact with each in turn and offered a smile.

There were more announcements, a final prayer, and the meeting broke for the serving of the noon meal. Tazz had no chance to get close to Colena, as she was mingling with the other women and seemed right popular. Once the ladies had set out the edibles, the children were served first, then everyone formed a line and began to fill tin plates with food. Millie was at the punch bowl, pouring drinks for each person. Tazz was at the back of the line when two shadows darkened his path.

'He's the one,' Peters growled, blocking his way. 'I recognize his fancy Stetson.'

Boyle cornered him from the other side and pushed his big chest up against him.

'You've got a big nose, stranger.' His tone was menacing, his pungent breath right in Tazz's face. 'Mayhaps we ought to squash it for you!'

Tazz displayed a disarming smile. 'Boys, I apologize for being on the aggressive side last night. I had no idea what I was getting into – that's a fact.'

'Oh, yeah?' Boyle sneered.

'That woman really gave me what-for after we mixed it up. She lectured to me about interfering and commenced to cuss me all the way to the boarding house. I swear, I haven't had a tongue-lashing like that since the first time I let slip a profanity where my ma could hear. We'd all three have been better off not to have crossed her path.'

'You don't say?' Boyle asked, his scowl turning into a curious frown.

'Believe me, I done you fellows a favor,' Tazz continued. 'I'd sooner pry open the mouth of an angry grizzly bear and pull his hind teeth than walk that gal home again.'

Peters grinned. 'A real hell-cat, huh?'

'The likes of which I never met before,' Tazz replied. 'I'm telling you, she scalded my hide all the way home. And she's college-educated, so she used two-dollar words for the most part.'

His amiable manner displaced the belligerent character of the two men. Boyle began to chuckle.

'Maybe we was the lucky ones, only taking a mud-bath.'

'Yeah,' Peters agreed. 'I'm beginning to think we got the best of it last night.'

'Take my word, fellows. You both owe me a drink for rescuing you.'

'She sure enough come on all uppity,' Boyle proclaimed. 'Didn't figure her to be the new banker.'

'I reckon she'll give you boys a smile and extend you both credit, before I'll even get the time of day from her. Talk about a nasty temper!'

'I kin imagine,' Boyle said between fits of laughter. 'Tote that bag fer me, sonny! Don't be getting no smudges on my things!'

'And don't go spitting none of your tobacco around me,' Peters contributed. 'It ain't mannerly!'

Boyle continued: 'Straighten your shoulders, boy! When you slouch like that you look like an overgrown ape!'

Tazz joined in with them. 'Even called me a Penance Paladin, whatever that is.'

'Bet a paladin is something like a stray dog what's not wanted,' Boyle said.

Tazz nodded. 'Sounds about right . . . 'cept I wouldn't talk to a dog the way she done me.'

'I can hear her now.' Peters used a mocking voice. 'If you must address me, do it properly and use them fancy four-syllable words. I'm a college-educated lady. You talk to and treat me as such!'

Boyle slapped Tazz on the back. 'Yeah, man! You sure got the worst of it!'

'I'll say!' Peters was nearly doubled up from laughter. 'We owe you a debt, mister. You sure saved our hides!'

'Come on over to the table,' Tazz offered. 'I'll buy you boys a lemonade.'

Boyle raised a hand. 'No thanks. That stuff would curdle last night's beer and I'd be sick for a week.'

'Me too,' Peters agreed.

'Sure, leave me here by myself,' Tazz joked. 'What if that she-cat decides to tear into me again? I could use some protection!'

'God give you two legs, son.' Boyle smirked. 'Use them to skedaddle with!'

The two men roared with laughter, so loud that many heads turned to see what was so funny. As the two men headed for the barn door, Tazz noticed the three of them had earned the attention of Colena Hawthorn. He was smiling for the benefit of Boyle and Peters, until he was struck by the icy look in her eyes.

Now what? he wondered. Why the hostile glare?

Colena returned to serving and Tazz was unable to catch her looking his way again. He fell into line next to a couple of talkative miners. By the time he reached the table another woman had taken over serving and Colena had taken a seat on a bench. The man who planted himself next to her was the gent from the pulpit. It appeared Phil was quizzing her about her background or the bank. Rather than working on a plate of food, he had a pad of folded paper in his hand and continually scribbled down notes.

Tazz needed a few minutes alone with Colena. He had to introduce himself properly and explain he was here to work with her. There was also the little matter of her stealing his horse and clothes. He wished to get the awkward incident dismissed, so they could start fresh.

However, the chance did not present itself. Tolken remained glued to her side and appeared happy to stay for the duration of the day. Who could blame him? Colena was pretty, she was a new arrival in town, and she was news. With the constant introductions of other curious people, Tazz gave up the idea of trying to speak to her in private. He would have to wait for another time.

CHAPTER FOUR

Tazz looked for Colena at breakfast, but she didn't show. He was beginning to wonder if the gal ever ate. He got spruced up in his store-bought suit, dusted off his hat and put on his polished boots. Then he began the walk to the bank. He stopped to pick up a copy of the local newsletter and arrived to discover a CLOSED sign on the locked door. Sticking the paper into his back pocket, he put his knuckles to the door and waited.

A small man hobbled over, unlocked and opened the door. He jerked his thumb at the notice.

'If you don't know how to read, ask someone!' he said bluntly. 'We ain't open for business.'

'I'm not here to open an account, Shorty.'

The little guy straightened and glared up at Tazz. 'The name's not Shorty! It's Doby Grant . . . clerk and teller of this here bank.'

'Yeah, well, I'm Tazz Spencer . . . *vice-president* of this here bank!'

Doby continued to frown, as if the words took time to sink in. Then a smile cracked his face and he began to laugh.

'You're the new vice-president?'

'That's right.'

Doby surprised him by reaching out and taking his hand. He began to shake it up and down like it was a pump handle and he was dying of thirst.

'Man, oh, man! Am I glad to meet you!'

Tazz was stunned by the rapid turn around.

'I don't get it.'

'You're my savior!' Doby said. 'I was scared to death I was going to be Miss Hawthorn's only whipping-boy, but now you're here!'

'You're saying the gal is a tyrant?'

'Heck no!' He kept his voice hushed. 'A tyrant would be a saint alongside her. She's determined to show her father she can make a go of this bank . . . even if she has to build its success upon the abused and broken bodies of men like me and you!'

Colena took notice that Tazz was taking up her clerk's valuable time. She came storming over to the door with daggers of flame leaping from her eyes.

'What do you want, cowboy?' She verbally attacked Tazz. 'I'm not looking for someone to walk me home, and we are closed!'

'I read the sign,' he answered drily. 'I appreciate your using a small word.'

Her teeth came together and she hissed the next question: 'So why are you here?'

Tazz grinned. 'I didn't know who you were Saturday night, ma'am.'

Her breath appeared to catch in her throat and a naked guilt flooded her attractive features. She obviously realized he knew she was the one who had robbed him.

'And,' Tazz drawled on, 'you were a little too occu-
pied to get close to at the meeting yesterday. We need
to have us a little talk.'

'Talk?' she repeated inanely. 'I – I don't know what
you mean.'

'Are you sure about that?' he asked, his words drip-
ping with sarcasm.

'I – I'm afraid not.' Her reply was forced. 'Whatever
do you want with me?'

'I'm Tazz Spencer,' he said, showing a smile, 'your
new vice-president.'

The news hit Colena in the face like a well-thrown
tomato.

'Y – you . . . I – I . . . It's . . .'

She sputtered, as if trying to comprehend his words.
'You're what?'

'Yep.' He continued the amiable simper, 'Your pa,
Knute, he hired me to help you put this here bank into
the black. I reckon it won't be but a few weeks and we
can throw the red ink out altogether.'

Colena looked as if she had swallowed a bug! She
rotated about to the clerk.

'Doby, go in and continue the transfer work with Mr
Myerson. We were in the process of listing the accounts
receivable in alphabetical order.'

Doby was respectful. 'Certainly, Miss Hawthorn.'

'Mr Spencer,' she returned to Tazz, 'we need to
speak in private.'

'Whatever you say, ma'am,' he said comfortably.
'You're the boss.'

Colena waited for Doby to limp into the manager's
office and shut the door behind him. Then she led Tazz

smartly over to the furthermost corner of the room. When she reached the wall, she spun about and glared at him with a heated gaze.

'What kind of dastardly trick is this?' she demanded to know. 'What qualifies you to be vice-president of my bank?'

'I don't believe there's anything dastardly going on.'

She continued to scowl. 'I don't understand! Why would my father hire you to such a position?'

'You'd have to ask him.'

She gnashed her teeth angrily. 'Are you familiar with accounting procedures and compiling interest?'

'Not in the slightest.'

'How about simple bookkeeping? Can you do that?'

'I never was much for writing things down, but I am a good judge of character.'

She was quickly becoming exasperated. 'If you know nothing of accounting or bank procedures, how can you perform the necessary duties as a bank vice-president?'

'According to your pa, my part is more to handle security and bring in new business. I believe he had it in mind for me to persuade some of the nearby miners and ranchers to put their money in our bank.'

She cringed at his term *our bank*! 'I'm sorry,' she said, 'but I don't foresee the need of your services, Mr, Spencer.'

'No?'

'I didn't require your help to handle those two ruffians Saturday night, nor to traverse the mud *en route* to the boarding-house.'

'If you say so.'

'I do!' She snapped the words. 'And I neither require nor do I want any help from you concerning my bank.'

He shrugged off her argument. 'Sorry to hear you feel that way, ma'am.'

'You're sorry?'

'Yup,' he didn't budge, 'because your pa guaranteed me three months' work here in Penance. If it don't pan out, he said he would find me another place in the company.'

Colena lifted her hands and used her fingers to rub her temples.

'I . . .' She had to pause long enough to clear her throat. 'I don't know if I can abide by his agreement.'

'Your pa and I shook hands on it.' Then, as she was reluctant to continue, Tazz bore into her with a startling frankness. 'Besides which, I reckon dismissing me without giving me a chance would be about the same as robbing a man out in the wilderness.' As her expression transformed into a mixture of guilt and shock, he continued: 'It would be about as low and underhanded as to leave a guy naked and afoot.'

Colena's face lit up like a red lantern. She visibly squirmed under his intense stare.

'Y – you know?' She barely breathed the words.

'Without even having to sneak a peek at your pretty pink bloomers.'

That news item snapped her head upward. She stared at him in alarm.

'How much of me *did* you see?' She pointed an accusing finger at him. 'Your hat was down over your eyes. You could not possibly have seen my . . .' she gulped hard, 'my face!'

He lifted his hands in a calming gesture. 'Not to worry, ma'am,' he assured her quickly. 'I only caught a glimpse of your fancy drawers . . . nothing else.'

'Then how . . . ?'

'I suspect you could try and mask the normal sound of your voice, cover up your wiles in a dozen heavy petticoats, and I'd still have known it was you.'

'Pray tell, how could you manage that?'

'It has to do with vanilla,' he said, allowing himself a smile. 'You had just bathed in the stream and used something with the scent of vanilla for your hair. When I carried you home the other night, I detected the same aroma. It was concealed some by the rain and dust from traveling, but it was the very same.'

'I see.'

'You also have a distinctive way of talking, ma'am. Being educated, you don't sound like most ordinary girls.'

'Why didn't you confront me about this when I arrived Saturday night?'

'Like I said, I only come to figure who you were for certain when they introduced you at the meeting. Once I heard the name Hawthorn, I knew you were the one.'

'What does my name have to do with this?'

'I had already traced you back to the bank. If it hadn't been for the run-in with the Akins bunch and this here job offer, I would have been around to see you.'

'You mean to arrest me?'

'No such a thing.'

She frowned. 'You would have been within your rights! I should think you would be incensed over the incident.'

58

'Walking ten miles in riding-boots takes some of the starch out of a man's backbone, ma'am.' He lifted his shoulders in a shrug. 'Plus, I can understand why you might not have been in a real trusting mood, after your encounter with the Akins boys.'

'I'm relieved you understand.'

'Yes, ma'am.'

She sighed. 'Very well, Mr Spencer. It appears we are going to be working together – at least, for the three months my father promised you. After that, I'm sure he will find a more suitable position for you elsewhere.'

'If you say so, Miss Hawthorn.'

She moistened her lips, as if anticipating being kissed. The unconscious act was enough to stir the soul of a man six weeks in the grave.

'I do apologize about the way I handled the situation at the river,' she said at last. 'I should have asked for your help, instead of knocking you from your saddle and stealing your horse and clothes.'

'It was mostly my fault for being careless.' He excused her behavior. 'The Akins boys could have forced you to call out for help. Had that been the case, I'd be plunking harp strings and singing hymns up above, instead of being a bank vice-president.'

Mention of the title once again caused her to frown.

'I'm still not comfortable with the idea of you serving as vice-president.'

'That's OK. You'll get used to me.'

'It has nothing to do with you personally. I'm certain my father was only seeking to provide for my welfare. I understand his concern, but I don't need a bodyguard.'

'He said I was to handle security for the bank,' Tazz said. 'But he didn't say anything about looking after you. I didn't even know I'd be working for a woman.'

'Really?'

'On my honor as vice-president,' he avowed, with an upward curl of his lips.

'I suppose you would be a good choice to contact the nearby ranchers and visit the different mines in the region. Your appointment offers a podium for speaking to the numerous owners and ranchers about coming into the bank.'

'I can do that, but you won't have a shortage of customers for the first few days.'

She pinched her brows together. 'What are you talking about?'

'Anyone who reads the town flyer will be coming to have a look at you. Phil Tolken wrote you up as a big story.' Tazz reached around to his back pocket and withdrew the folded newsletter. 'I figured a proper educated woman like you would read the newspaper from cover to cover in about five seconds flat.'

She snatched the paper out of his hand and stared at the article. As she scanned over the words, her grip tightened to wrinkle the sheet of paper.

'Says some flattering things there,' Tazz offered.

'So I see.' She bit off the words. 'He asserts: "Miss Hawthorn is the only woman bank manager in the entire country. She is cerebral, charming and attractive".' She crushed the paper between her hands. 'He dwells upon my physical attributes, but not one blessed thing about my credentials!'

'Ain't that what *cerebral* means? Or does it have to do

60

with angels?' At her scowl, he continued: 'Anyway, look-ing at it from a business point of view, ma'am, few men out here care about your education. Being a woman is enough to draw them into the bank. You'll have them lined up out into the street tomorrow to see you up close.'

She whirled about and put her back to Tazz.

'I want people to bank with us because I'm capable. I want to earn their esteem for my competency at handling finances. I abhor the idea of them only coming to see me because I'm a woman.'

'Not an ordinary woman either,' Tazz contributed. 'Like the paper says, you're on the attractive side too.'

'Thank you, Mr Tolken.' She jeered the newsman's words. 'He destroyed any chance I had for earning the respect of these men.'

'It can work to your advantage,' Tazz countered.

'And what advantage is that?'

'When you meet the men face to face, you'll have a chance to explain your credentials. Them fellers what have any smarts are going to see you as an intelligent sort.'

'How comforting.'

'Listen, ma'am, even when there's only one bakery in town, they put out a sign to advertise their bread or pastries.'

'You're implying this is advertising?' She spun back to face Tazz. 'Is that what I am – window dressing?'

'I was trying to make a point.'

'Yes, I see your point, Mr Spencer.' She set her teeth. 'Would you also suggest I wear beguiling attire? Perhaps something to accent my feminine attributes?'

He could see she was being cynical, so he displayed a roguish simper.

'A skirt which allows a glimpse of those fancy pink under-trousers might be a good idea.' He winked at her. 'They sure caught my eye.'

She swung her open palm at his face. Tazz, with a swift move, caught hold of her wrist, preventing the slap.

'Whoa!' he said quickly. 'I was only funning.'

She yanked her hand free of his grip. 'I don't see any humor in the situation, Mr Spencer! We are promoting a service here, not selling a pound of flesh!'

'All I'm saying is what's done is done. Like it or not, you're going to have men from all over the country riding here to get a look at you. You can take advantage of it, or you can hole up and refuse any visitors. You give the say-so and I'll stop each man at the door. I'll tell them you ain't of the mind to have no curiosity types bothering you. If they ain't got a pocketful of money, you ain't interested.'

Colena was still simmering, but Tazz had made a valid point. The news was already out. She could either use the article to her advantage, or she could make a fool of herself and destroy any hope of having decent public relations with potential customers.

'I suppose we will have to deal with the curiosity seek-ers.'

'I was in a mining town one time where men stood in line for several hours just to have themselves a look at a proper lady. There's been a couple men who made more money charging miners to look at or speak to their wives than they did from digging for gold. It's a fact, men so far away from a real town get lonely for the sight of a lady.'

'I'm surprised you think of me as a lady,' she admitted. 'After taking your horse and clothes, I might have presupposed you would label me with a different title.'

'We've been over that once,' he assured her. 'I ain't the kind to hold a grudge.'

Colena was serene. 'Perhaps you aren't as ill-suited for the job as I first assumed.'

'Would that be one of them there left-handed compliments?'

She finally cracked a genuine smile. 'Possibly.'

'Well, whatever you need, I'm your man,' he pledged. 'We vice-presidents are always willing to help.'

Colena returned to the business at hand. 'Have you looked over the bank?'

'I arrived the middle of the week and come by for a look-see,' he said.

'And what are your suggestions for security?'

'The safe wouldn't slow down a robber with a team and wagon. A couple strong men could pick it up and haul the thing right off.'

'Yes, its weight is listed on a label plate as only four hundred pounds.'

'I was talking to a bricklayer at the saloon,' Tazz told her. 'He says we could get us a load of bricks and mortar the safe into the rear wall. It would make it more like a regular vault and prevent a robber from throwing a rope over it and dragging it away.'

'That's a good idea,' she agreed. 'Anything else?'

'There are bars on the windows, but the door is a light-weight wood. A man could put his shoulder to it and knock it off its hinges. I think we should either buy a more solid door or add a few steel bars.'

'There have been few bank robberies in this part of the country.'

'Yeah, but there's no real law in Penance. It makes us a little more inviting.'

'I'll consider replacing the door,' she agreed. Then, when he didn't add more, she gave her head a slight bob. 'I'll expect you to report to me each morning before we open for business and I will outline your duties.'

'It's going to be a real pleasure working with you, ma'am,' he told her.

The lady's cheeks grew pink. 'As for today, you can spend the day visiting with prospective customers. If I don't see you back at Millie's place, I'll expect you here at the bank in the morning.'

He made a quick farewell, picked up his horse and spent the day riding about the countryside. He met several ranchers and spoke to them about using the bank to handle their money or even taking out a loan. The small talk and travel caused him to arrive back in town too late for supper at the boarding-house. He took time to rub down his mare and see to it she was fed and watered. For an evening meal, he decided to patronize the Open Pit saloon.

As taverns went, the Open Pit had a little of everything. There was a twenty-foot oak bar along one wall, a number of gaming-tables, and a small stage at the back. For those wanting something to eat, there were several tables in one corner for serving up meals. A couple customers were there, having after-dinner smokes and coffee. Tazz took a chair at an empty table and waited for service.

Being a Monday night, the place was pretty slow. He knew, from a previous visit, the place offered an entertainer, ReAnn Gannon, the daughter of the Open Pit owner. There was also an old gent who played piano in the evenings. ReAnn seemed a big help to her father. She waited tables all day and, most evenings, she would serve up a song or dance or both, depending on her mood and the crowd. She was a local favorite, not only due to her rather nice voice and physically attractive features, but simply because she was female. Tazz was pleased to discover she was serving tables in the eating section.

'You're new in town,' she greeted him. He noted she was a little on the fleshy side, but it added a softness to her otherwise robust body. She was ample-bosomed, with rounded hips and, having seen her dance, he knew she had very nice legs. Her features were those of a baby-face, pleasingly chubby cheeks and full, pouting lips. She had large brown eyes, with the first hint of lines at the corners, undoubtedly from squinting and keeping late hours in a room full of smoke. Dusky-blond streaks were throughout her long sandy-brown hair, and she had a rather large mouth, a physical characteristic which Tazz thought often denoted a good singing voice.

'You tending tables this time of night?'

She gave a subtle lift to her shoulders. 'I'm stuck doing about everything around here. The usual woman who helps us is home with a sick kid.'

'Too bad for her,' he said, displaying his smile, 'but lucky for me.'

ReAnn had certainly heard every compliment or charming line there was, but she acknowledged his flattery with a slight upturn of her mouth and a twinkle in her eyes.

'We've got left-over stew from the dinner special or we can toss a steak on the fire.'

'Steak, just shy of being burnt, and a bushel of tatters ought to do me just fine.'

'Be a few minutes,' she said. 'I was helping clean up.'

'I can get by on the left-over stew, if it's going to be extra work for you.'

'No, only warning you it'll take fifteen to twenty minutes.'

'I've got plenty of time.'

She rotated around and trudged into the kitchen. Her heavy steps were contrary to when he'd seen her snappy routines when she pranced about on stage. Despite being of a full figure, ReAnn was a lissom and proficient dancer. She could dazzle the male audience with a swirl of petticoats and an occasional high kick – which often drew the toss of a few coins up onto the stage. She was obviously worn out from a long day.

Instead of busying herself cleaning tables, ReAnn returned and sat down opposite Tazz. He was surprised by the action, but offered up his best smile.

'You put in long hours.'

'My pa had me kicking up my heels and dancing to earn money from the time I first learned to walk. I've grown used to it over the years.'

'This place wouldn't do half as much business without you.'

She gave him a critical once-over. 'So you're Tazz Spencer.'

He blinked at her knowing his name. 'That's right. How'd you know?'

She tipped her head, as if to shrug. 'Word gets around. Phil was in earlier. From the way he talked, you will be his major news story tomorrow. He said you'd come to Penance to be the strong-arm at the bank.'

His surprise was now a frown. 'I did hire on to work at the bank.'

'You don't look like the man I pictured from his description,' she told him, candidly surveying him from head to foot. 'I would have expected you to be about as hard as a railroad spike, maybe with a wild head of hair down to your shoulders and the glint of steel in your eyes.' With a smile, 'You have rather nice eyes.'

'I'm right proud you think so, Miss Gannon.'

'Ray,' she said. 'My friends call me Ray.'

'Again I'm proud to think we're going to be friends ... Ray,' he said, trying to remember the last time he had called a lady by her first name.

'So, what kind of a name is Tazz?'

'My mother was a Russian immigrant. Her maiden name was Tosya Zhenechka. My folks put together her first and last name and came up with Tazz.'

'I kind of wondered about it. I'd never heard it used before.'

'I've taken some ribbing about my handle, especially when still going to school.'

Ray sighed. 'I never got to attend school much. Pa kept us moving around, following the silver or gold strikes. We first started out with him and my mother selling goods to miners, then we got a cook wagon and began serving meals.'

'How about your knack for entertaining?'

There was an upturn at the corners of her mouth. 'I picked up a little here and there. Pa took me to see a show in Denver once, back when I was still a tiny tot. I learned myself to dance, and Bennie, our piano man, he taught me the words to a few songs.'

'I've been around a good many saloons and an actual theater or two,' Tazz told her. 'You're easily as good as most of those professional types.'

That caused a genuine smile to appear. 'Really?'

'Yes, ma'am. You've a natural way of being one with the music.'

'If I was younger, I might consider trying to make myself a career . . . you know, the theater and all.'

'You're not all that old.'

'I'm going on twenty-four,' she said. 'Besides which, I've been seeing Kip Partee, the man who runs the company store. He claims he is going to take me away from here and we can be married one day – maybe another year or two.'

'He only *claims* he's going to take you away?'

'I'm not giving him my answer until he can promise me a home of my own. I don't want to prance about and sing for coins in a saloon. If I sing and dance, I want it to be at a real theater. As for marrying him, if he wants me, he will have to support me.'

'Sounds like a fair offer to me.'

She laughed. 'He whines every time I mention the terms. I don't think he's ever saved a penny in his life.'

'Maybe he never had reason enough before.'

'Yeah, maybe.'

'I haven't met Partee yet.'

'You're in competition with him now,' she said, displaying an odd sort of smile.

He wondered if she was referring to the bank or spoke in regards to her. 'Reckon our trails will cross one of these next days,' he said, allowing the matter to pass without comment. 'I've been in his store, but there was an elderly gal watching the place.'

'She's a maiden aunt. She tends to his house chores and helps at the store.'

'So, if you was to marry him, you wouldn't care to help him run the store?'

Ray stared off into space for a moment. 'I'd like to move to a big city, with a house close enough so's I can walk to the nearby shops. I'd also like some nice clothes and maybe a little expensive perfume.' She gave a negative shake of her head. 'I don't want my kids growing up in mining towns, running around like little beggars, dirty and barefoot. They will attend school and be smart. They'll become upstanding citizens.'

'Sounds like a good plan.'

She seemed to remember she had company. 'It's only a dream.'

'Dreams can come true sometimes.'

His remark put another smile on her face, but just then her father bellowed:

'Ray! Get off your lazy backside and tend to business!'

'Yeah, Pa!' she replied obediently and rose up from the chair. She hesitated, another peculiar look in her eyes. Was it because she had told him a secret she had not intended, or was there something else?

'I'll check on your meal, Tazz. It should be about ready.'

'Thank you, Ray,' he said, 'but there's no hurry.'

She left him at the table and he wondered why she would show a special interest in him. Probably because she had spoken to the newspaper man and learned a little about him. She was likely curious about the new bankers.

There was another thought too. She could have been checking him out for her fiancé. If the bank was going to run competition to the store, concerning the handling of money for the miners, he might have wanted her to pick Tazz's brain. The flaw in that idea was the fact she had asked practically nothing about the bank, not even his own background. No, there were other mysteries about ReAnn, things he did not yet understand. He would have to bide his time until he learned more about her.

CHAPTER FIVE

Having eaten a big meal late the previous night, Tazz skipped breakfast. He washed up and shaved, then ran a comb through his hair and donned his newly purchased black suit of clothes. A clean white shirt peaked out from under the fork-tailed jacket. He added a string tie and strapped on his gun. Finished, he took a moment to check his appearance in the mirror and was satisfied that the jacket, by hanging a few inches below his waist, kept the gun on his hip from being all that noticeable.

'About as dandy as a back-East politician,' he appraised himself.

The street was passable, except for a few remaining muddy spots. Tazz arrived at the walkway in front of the row of saloons and encountered two or three of the locals. It took only a glance at their faces before he realized something had changed. A swamper from one of the saloons stopped work and stared at him with an odd expression. As he passed, he muttered a 'good morning, sir.' Then, when he approached one of the store owners, the man scurried out of his way, acting fearful for his life.

A bit further along, he saw the boy who delivered the *Daily Flyer*, the newsletter Phil Tolken put out. Tazz paused to reach into his pocket for a coin, but the boy's face grew suddenly bright, his eyes wide and filled with awe.

'No charge today, Mr Spencer,' he said quickly, shoving a paper at him. 'No, sir, your money ain't no good today.'

Tazz accepted a free copy of the paper and stared at the youngster. The boy continued to look at Tazz as if he were seven feet tall and near as wide.

What the Sam Hill is going on here? he wondered. Ain't any of these people ever seen a man wearing a new store-bought suit before?

A glance at the paper in his hand solved the puzzle. There was a picture of four bodies, all laid out side by side, a photograph he had seen before. It was the Akins bunch, displayed under the heading: HERO OF ROUSING SHOOT-OUT TO CO-RUN LOCAL BANK.

The story went on to detail how Tazz had taken on four bank robbers in a thrilling gunfight and mowed them all down. He hardly recognized himself in print. The man described in the article was fearless and invincible, standing against four desperate killers with guns blazing. He had gone down in a hail of gunfire, but not before he sent the last of the Akin clan to their graves.

Tazz crushed the paper between his hands. So that was the game! He was to bring in new clients, handle difficult situations and be in charge of security! Yeah, right!

His blood began to boil. All Knute and Colena wanted was his reputation. With no law in Penance, they figured his name would be enough to dissuade any trouble or would-be bandits. He took determined strides down the walk, until he reached the front of the bank. It would not open for business for another hour, but Doby saw him approach and was there to open the door for him.

'Good morning, Mr Spencer,' he offered.

'The boss here?' Tazz asked, entering the building.

Doby seemed a little confused by the title. 'The manager is in her office.'

Tazz didn't say thanks or bob his head in acknowledgment – not even *get out of my way!* He stalked across the room and jerked open the door. Without knocking or waiting for an invite, he stepped into the office and slammed the door behind him.

A trace of annoyance swept over Colena's face, but it was abruptly disguised by her professional demeanor.

'Yes, Mr Spencer?'

He tossed the crumpled up newsletter onto her desk. 'You know about this?'

She frowned at the disrespectful action, but smoothed out and glanced at the paper. A red tint came into her cheeks and she glowered up at Tazz with smoldering eyes.

'*Co-run* the bank?' She read only the headline. 'What kind of nonsense is that!'

'I'm more concerned about the picture.'

She took a second look at the page.

'It would appear Mr Tolken acquired a copy of the photograph from Denver,' she acknowledged.

'Was this your idea or your father's doing?' he demanded to know.

73

Colena's expression turned cold and she half-rose from her chair. 'Don't use that master-servant tone of voice with me, Mr Spencer. I am not a Saturday-night drunk to be intimidated by your prowess with a gun. I happen to be your employer.'

'I didn't hire on to be a target for every young whelp looking to get himself a reputation, Miss Hawthorn. This here story makes me sound like a gunman for hire, a killer who is no longer hiding behind a badge. It even goes so far as to warn any want-a-be gun-slicks to keep out of Penance!'

'Perhaps you are overreacting.'

'Do you know how this place came to be called Penance, lady?' He was still boiling. 'It's because, when they started mining these hills, no regular miners dared work up here. There were constant Indian attacks, claim jumpers behind every bend, and bandits and thieves hit about every shipment of gold before it reached the smelter. The only way to recruit men for digging was to pay their fines and get them from jail or prison! Men working here were doing penance for their crimes or deeds, Miss Hawthorn. That's where the town got its name.'

'What has that got to do with the news article?'

'It has everything to do with my survival! These mines are still filled by a fair number of criminals, those convicted of everything from murder to robbery and any other crime you can think of. Writing something like this is not a way to prevent them from taking up a gun against me, it's a challenge to do exactly that!'

A glimmer of comprehension seeped into Colena's expression. 'I am beginning to understand your concern, but I don't see what can we do about it now.'

'There is nothing *we* can do about it,' he said. 'As for myself, I've a mind to pack my gear and shag my carcass out of town.'

Colena pushed back her chair and stood up straight. A minute alarm sprang into her eyes.

'You can't do that!'

'And why not?'

'Because you made a commitment to this bank. You accepted a position for a minimum of three months!'

'I should think you'd jump at the chance to be rid of me.'

'That's beside the point,' she declared. 'With this article, it will be common knowledge around town that you were hired to work at the bank. How would it look if you up and quit before we even open the doors?'

He grunted. 'I see how it is. There's no need for concern about my life, but you wouldn't want to disappoint any customers who might expect a notorious gunman to be protecting their money.'

She lifted her chin. 'Exactly.'

He strode to the edge of the desk so he could look down at the woman. Colena was no wilting persimmon. She came around to stand toe to toe with him, hands on her hips, jaw thrust out in defiance – a field mouse willfully confronting an alley-cat. It was a contest, a measure of strength and power. Each of them maintained eye contact, daring the other to blink first.

Tazz stared into her scintillating lime-green eyes and was mesmerized by the dark, inviting twin pools. Her stubborn defiance caused a slight gathering of her neatly trimmed eyebrows and firmly compressed lips.

He was close enough to detect the sweet scent of the vanilla fragrance she had used when she had last bathed and shampooed her hair. He had intended to subjugate her with his size and male dominance, but she was not a woman to be intimidated.

He was the one to speak, ending the glaring match.

'You don't give a hang about my life or anything else in the world other than this bank. Ain't that the truth?'

'You should cease using the word *ain't*,' she said evenly. 'It isn't tasteful grammar for a bank vice-president.'

'Oh, it ain't?'

'No,' she snapped, her face flushed with exasperation, 'it *ain't*!'

He could not maintain his staunch posture. Somehow, the way she threw the word *ain't* back into his face struck him as humorous. A tight grin sneaked its way into his expression.

'You've got a short fuse.'

'I'm a perfectionist when it comes to my work!'

'Yeah, I've commenced to figure as much about you.'

She took a step back and surveyed him from head to foot.

'I must admit, I am impressed by your attire. You at least present the appearance of a gentleman.'

Tazz didn't realize his hands had moved until he felt the soft flesh of Colena's shoulders beneath his fingers.

'I might look the part, but I sure don't feel like a gentleman around you.'

Colena visibly caught her breath, but replied:

'And why is that, Mr Spencer?'

He didn't reply in words. Involuntarily, he drew her

closer and his head came downward. He didn't think: it was a natural response, a primal urge which overruled his good senses. Before he realized what he was doing, his mouth covered her own.

Colena was obviously surprised at his action, so unprepared, in fact, she forgot to resist. It was several glorious seconds before she recovered her wits. At the slight pressure from her hands, Tazz released her.

Colena vocalized a soft 'ahem' and cleared her throat. Then she pivoted about, moved smartly back to her desk, positioned her chair carefully and took her seat. With a wholly unruffled appearance, she looked up at him.

'I expect you to fulfill your contract, Mr Spencer,' she stated directly. 'Should you decide to the contrary, I need to pass along the information to Mr Tolken. That way, he could print a retraction in tomorrow's newsletter.'

Tazz suffered a sense of wonder and confusion, but he salvaged enough sense to reply:

'Reckon I'll stick for a spell.' He shrugged. 'No need making a big deal out of becoming a target for every petty gunman in the country. After all, it's only my life.'

'Then it's settled,' she said, once more in total control of the situation. 'Perhaps you could screen the prospective customers who come to pay their respects today. I'm sure I won't have time for all of the curiosity seekers, the ones who only wish to gawk and exchange small talk. I need to occupy my time with those people who have a genuine interest in doing business.'

'I'll make an effort to root out the weeds and allow

only the best of the crop to take up your time, Miss Hawthorn.'

She remained polite and businesslike. 'Thank you, Mr Spencer. We can compare notes at the end of the day.'

'Yeah, OK,' Tazz mumbled, opening the door and leaving the room.

He was still dazed as he entered the main lobby of the bank. He saw Doby was at the teller window, counting the morning drawer. The man glanced up, but there was no indication he was interested in anything but making certain of each coin or bill.

'Fifteen minutes,' the old boy said, tipping his head in the direction of a clock on the wall. Without skipping a beat with his count, he added: 'I put a pen, ink and some paper on your desk, in case you wanted to write down information or the like. Miss Hawthorn's instructions were that she would be the one to take loan applications or handle any investment accounts, but I'm sure you'll have plenty to do too.'

'Yeah, thanks, Shorty,' he said, moving over to his desk. 'And if you need to leave the window long enough for a smoke or something, give a holler. I can stand back there and either confuse or socialize with the customers till you get back.'

Doby chuckled at his honesty. 'I'll remember, Mr Spencer.'

'Tazz is the handle I go by, Shorty. I ain't stuffy about titles.'

'I prefer Doby . . . Tazz,' he said, still smiling. 'But I must use your proper title in front of our customers. We must maintain proper social decorum.'

'Danged if you don't sound like our boss, using them fancy words.'

'If not for lack of material wealth,' Doby mused, 'I could have been a proper snob.'

Tazz laughed at his jest and wandered over to rest his haunch on what would be his desk. He had nothing to do until the doors were opened. However, several people had already gathered on the street. There was bound to be some curiosity about Colena. A female bank manager was about as scarce as a whiskey jug at a temperance rally.

His desk was situated behind a wood banister, which adjoined the teller counter and cordoned off the rear of the room. It was necessary for anyone going to Colena's office to pass by his desk via a gateway a few feet from his desk. She had privacy, whereas he did not, a preference which separated a bank president from the vice-president.

Oddly enough, he realized the question of his sticking it out had been settled by virtue of their office encounter. After kissing Colena, he couldn't very well toss in his chips and walk away. Quite the contrary. For another chance to kiss her honey-sweet lips, he would sure enough brave the fires of perdition!

He smiled at the memory, both amazed and baffled by her reaction to his kiss. She would have been within her rights to slap him silly for his impertinence, but she had returned the kiss instead. He might have thought she allowed him the favor to keep him working for her bank, except she had not wanted him there in the first place.

Either she was too surprised to react or she had some

mild interest in a passing romance. The question was, what came next? How did an ordinary man impress a woman like Colena? And how did one court a bank manager, one who was also his boss?

He shelved the concerns as Doby opened the door and the first customers began to enter the bank. From the number lined up, it was going to be a busy day.

Doby ushered out the final stragglers, then closed and locked the front door. For Tazz, it was the first moment of peace he'd had all day. He was hoarse from discussing the fight in Denver. No one was much interested in his job at the bank. Each wanted to hear the details of the lethal gunfight which had left four men dead. He had repeated a modest version of the story until he was sick of telling it.

'Well, I'm glad we're through the first day.' Colena spoke up from behind him.

He turned in his chair and rose stiffly to his feet. 'I reckon I palavered with over thirty people today,' he told her. 'There wasn't but four of them who opened accounts.'

'I interviewed eighteen customers,' she said. 'You did a good job of discerning those who had actual funds from those who wanted to borrow money.'

His chest puffed slightly. 'We do any good then, I mean financially?'

She looked over at Doby for the answer. He finished adding a sum of figures and then looked up.

'We took in a grand total of two hundred and twelve dollars,' he said. 'Most of those coming to the window had very little actual money. The majority of people in town use scrip for cash.' He set a tray with some money on the counter. 'The drawer is ready for you to check and put into the safe.'

'Very good, Doby. Mr Spencer will let you out.'

The teller picked up his hat and Tazz escorted him to the front door. He let Doby out and locked the door behind him. Then he approached Colena from behind and watched her count the cash drawer. Her nimble fingers were swift and sure, as she tallied the drawer. At last she glanced over her shoulder.

'What?' she asked.

'I reckon you know why Harcore Worthington uses scrip?' he said. 'His company store and saloons take scrip, because he owns them all.'

'Yes, I'm aware of his strategy,' she answered. 'Worthington uses the scrip in place of money, so he controls where and how his miners spend their money.'

'Yeah, well, we need to work out a deal with him to exchange scrip for cash money,' Tazz said. 'We can't do much business without the miners.'

'I have a meeting with Mr Worthington tonight to discuss a proposition,' she replied off-handedly. 'He invited me to dinner at his house.'

'Oh?' Tazz didn't like the sound of a private sit-down at the man's place. 'How did I miss seeing a guy enter the bank with a king's crown on his head?'

'He didn't come in person. An invitation was brought by a town runner.'

Tazz remembered seeing the kid who had given him the free newsletter. The boy had come by with a piece of paper in his hand. He hadn't stopped him from going to Colena's office, as he figured the boy was delivering something from Tolken or perhaps a letter from the mail. Now he knew it had been a mistake to let him pass.

'I don't suppose you want my company?'

Colena placed the money drawer into the safe and closed the door.

'I appreciate your concern, Mr Spencer, but I can take care of myself.'

'You don't know anything about Worthington.'

'Mrs Tolken gave me some background on him. He's a forty-year-old, self-made millionaire. He plans to build a smelter, as soon as the railroad lays tracks through the canyon. He owns the Mother Lode, the company store, and has the lease or title to every major business, except for Millie's boarding-house and the Open Pit tavern. Plus, he owns all of the housing for the miners, the livery stable, and the narrow-gauge railroad, which is used to haul ore out of the mine.'

Tazz snorted. 'That all?' he asked sourly. 'You mean he don't own the air? Is it still free to breathe, or is he going to impose some kind of tax for our inhaling it?'

'His support will be instrumental in making a go of the bank.' Colena ignored his sarcasm. 'I need for him to let us exchange scrip for currency.'

'He might not be willing to share the banking. He uses his own company store as a bank for his miners.'

'Yes,' she replied. 'I know. He's a shrewd man.'

Tazz disliked the way Colena's eyes lit up when she spoke of Worthington. So what if he was as rich as Midas? Money didn't make the man. Of course, Colena was a banker. Perhaps money was the only thing of primary importance to all bankers.

'I suppose you'll dress up real fine and entice the man with your comely manners and intelligent conversation?'

She lifted her chin. 'Mr Worthington expects to meet with a proper lady.'

'And to be successful, might you want also to use your feminine wiles on him?'

'I don't see why it should matter to you whether I sway the man's opinion with my intellect or by way of feminine charm.'

There was a sudden gnawing within his chest. He didn't know if it was anger, jealousy – maybe a healthy dose of both! Tazz cursed his insecurity. Those were stupid feelings for a man who had nothing to offer a woman. He could not compete financially or socially with the baron of Penance. He didn't care for the sensation, not one bit.

'I guess I should mention I also got myself an invite this evening,' he said.

The news produced a curious frown. 'From whom?'

'Miss Gannon, from the Open Pit saloon. She wants to talk about investments.'

The frown deepened. 'I don't recall speaking to her.'

'No,' Tazz replied, feeling a little better at her negative reaction to his news. 'She's one of those narrow-minded sorts who don't put any faith in a woman banker.'

'I see.' Colena's reply was hedged with frost. 'And what words of advice can you possibly offer her?'

He attempted to put a professional tone into his voice.

'If she really does have some money to invest, I'll discuss her options with you.'

'You're not having dinner with her – not publicly?' There was a trace of irritation in Colena's voice. 'I mean, the Gannon woman – she's a dance-hall girl.'

'Actually, she's an *entertainer* at the Open Pit.' He narrowed his gaze. 'Does her money look different, 'cause she don't wear a bustle?'

'My concern is how it might look – a representative from our bank, having a private dinner with a . . . a dove of the evening.'

He grinned inwardly at the rise of color into her cheeks.

'Miss Gannon doesn't entertain privately. She is a singer and dancer. Plus, she also serves tables, but that's it.'

'I stand corrected.' She remained haughty. 'But I still have reservations about people witnessing your patron-izing a woman from a saloon.'

'You're having a private dinner with the tin god, Worthington,' he countered. 'I don't expect there's much difference.'

'The difference is, I'm the bank manager. You . . . you are . . .' She sputtered angrily, as if searching for the proper term.

'Yeah?' he prodded her.

'You're only here as a curiosity,' she blurted out in a huff. 'You're a celebrity, because you killed four other men in a gunfight. You are more comparable to an amusement at a county fair than a banker!'

Her brusque statement stung.

'Nice to know where I stand. For a little while today, I thought I might actually be doing a suitable job. Funny, the notion a man gets about his worth. I'm sorry

84

to be nothing more than an attraction in your freak show.'

The rush of crimson again flooded Colena's face. 'I didn't mean . . .'

But Tazz didn't wait for her to cut him any deeper. He spun about and strode smartly to the door. The key was in the lock, so he let himself out. When he shut the door, Colena was still standing in the middle of the room.

CHAPTER SIX

Standing next to his horse, hidden back in the trees, Tazz felt as if he was wearing a badge again. It was wrong to spy on Colena, but he pacified his conscience by telling himself he was duty-bound to protect his boss.

Worthington's enormous house was built like a fortress, surrounded by four-foot-high stone walls on three sides. The wood siding was freshly stained. Brightly lit chandeliers glowed from within its high-arched windows, and the main exterior twin doors were massive and ornamented like those of a church. The house had a huge front porch, enclosed by a decorated iron-rod railing, with a table and chairs for sitting out and enjoying the coolness of the evening air. To the front was an open yard, with an huge barn and tool-shed to one side, a bunkhouse and food-cellar to the other.

Tazz was impressed by the rock-laden courtyard and paved road, which ran from the house up to the main trail. Everything on Worthington's place spoke of money and wealth, including the fancy barouche parked at the front of the house. Sometimes called a brett or caleche, it was as fancy a carriage as he had ever

seen outside of the streets of Denver. It had been the
transport for Colena from the boarding-house.

He grunted his contempt. Worthington had not
called for the lady himself. He had sent a driver to fetch
her, as if he was too much like aristocracy to leave his
mansion.

And it probably impressed her!

The moon rose in the evening sky, full and bright,
illuminating the land, until the world was an assortment
of hazy shadows and undefined objects. The leaves
rustled in the trees from a slight breeze and the sound
of night creatures stirred the silence. There was the
buzz of a beetle, the constant chirp of a pair of noisy
birds and the occasional whinny of a horse in the
distant corrals.

His little mare shifted from resting one foot to resting on the other, patiently waiting for Tazz to grow
weary of his vigil. She was the same animal which
Colena had stolen from him. And she was the steadfast
horse from whose back Tazz had fought the gun battle
with the Akin clan. A few moments passed and the
horse shifted its weight again.

'I know,' Tazz spoke to the mare, 'me too. I reckon
I'm wasting our time.'

He was on a fool's errand. Worthington might try to
woo the satin bloomers off Colena, but he wouldn't force
the issue. Tazz had met the man during his travels to the
nearby ranches and mines. He recognized Worthington
as a regular dandy, well-heeled, practically oozing
manners and culture. He was elegant – probably considered handsome and distinguished to womenfolks. A man
like him would have no need to try and force from a

woman what most of them would offer willingly.

The mare snorted and stomped at a pesky night fly.

'Yeah, you're right,' Tazz said. 'We might as well call it a night.' Besides which, it would have made him more miserable to see Colena and Worthington together on the porch. What if she allowed him to kiss her?

He blanked the ugly notion from his brain. If he allowed himself to think along those lines, he might forget himself and storm the house to escort Colena home . . . with or without her permission. If he were to act in such an uncivilized manner, he could forget his position as vice-president or the lady's ever speaking to him again.

He returned to town, put his horse away for the night, then wandered over to the Open Pit and bought himself a beer. He arrived as Ray was crooning a sweet melody. Planting himself at a vacant table, he once more concluded she wasn't half-bad.

'You're one of the new bankers in town, aren't you?' a man asked, sitting down next to him without an invite.

Tazz rotated enough to look at him. Flat-crowned hat, dark hair grown down over his ears, with bushy eyebrows and a thick but neatly trimmed mustache. He was attired in a dressy black suit, more stand-outish than the one Tazz wore to the bank. He also had himself a pearl-handled Colt on his hip. He appeared a couple inches shorter than Tazz's own six foot, but was lean and fit in appearance.

'That's right,' Tazz replied. 'You a professional gambler?'

The man laughed. 'Kip Partee. I run the company store for Mr Worthington.'

Tazz stuck out his hand. 'I've been over there a couple times for supplies.'

Kip shook hands and sat back to study Tazz. 'So you're the man who took on four gunmen during a bank robbery?'

'Sounds like more of a feat than it was,' Tazz answered modestly. 'I just happened to arrive as they were coming out of the bank. I had luck and right on my side.'

'Luck I can deal with. I'll take the edge on the draw over being right any time.'

Tazz was quick to change the direction of their conversation.

'Miss Gannon mentioned the two of you might team up and pull in double-harness one of these days.'

Partee smiled, but it was more of a wary circumspection than a genuine smile.

'We've discussed a possible future. You thinking about cutting yourself into my game?'

'She seems a right good catch, Partee, but she strikes me as having a lot of spirit and a mind of her own. I don't think I could handle that much woman.'

Partee chuckled, satisfied with the answer. 'What about the banker lady? I met her when she stopped by to have me order a new hat from Denver. She's quite a looker.'

Tazz gave his shoulders a shrug. 'I never paid it much mind. She's my boss.'

'Yeah, right.'

Tazz grinned. 'Well, truthfully, I did notice she is a cut above average.'

'There's a story around about how you took up for

the lady against Boyle and Peters the night she arrived in town.' His words were nonchalant, but there was suspicion embedded in his eyes. 'One might think you are a hired bodyguard, rather than a banker.'

'It was only a misunderstanding between me and the boys,' Tazz answered. 'I thought they were a couple of drunks harrying a lady. We sorted it out the next day.'

'Lucky for you. Boyle is a mean man in a fight, and Peters likes to use a knife.'

'I'm glad we didn't have cause to mix it up. As it turned out, Miss Hawthorn wasn't all that pleased over my butting into her affairs.'

'I read Tolken's story about how her pa owns three banks.'

'His boy runs one for him over at Colorado Springs,' Tazz said. 'I don't know much about his overall finances, but the bank in Denver seems to do OK.'

'Family business,' Partee mused. 'Who better to trust than a son or daughter?'

Before Tazz could offer a reply, Ray came through the crowd. She nodded her head to acknowledge the compliments being tossed her way. She carried the gratuity cup, which had been passed around during her song.

'Wish I felt like dancing tonight,' she said, stirring the few coins around with her finger as she approached the two men. 'Nine pennies,' she complained. 'Hardly enough to buy a new ribbon for my Sunday-go-to-meeting hat.' With a sly simper at Tazz, 'Seems the men are more free with their money when I flash a little petticoat.'

'I'm not real fond of men having a look under your skirt,' Partee grumbled.

Tazz dug out a silver dollar and dropped it into her cup. 'They missed me during the passing of the hat,' he explained.

Ray beamed. 'See, Kip?' she said. 'I told you Tazz was a gentleman.'

The man didn't reply to her praise, but regarded him with a curious stare. 'There's a rumor your bank intends to exchange scrip at cash value. That right?'

'We should know by tomorrow. Miss Hawthorn is meeting with Mr Worthington tonight to talk about it. That would cut into your banking trade wouldn't it?'

'Other than an occasional loan, I don't do much banking.'

'Hate to take business away from you.'

'All of the profits from the store go to Mr Worthington.' Partee dismissed his concern. 'If you take the banking chores, it will actually make my job a little easier.'

'No hard feelings then?'

'Not a bit. If your bank exchanges scrip, maybe there will be a little real money around. I don't remember the last time I saw twenty dollars in cash.'

'And maybe I would get something in my cup besides pennies,' Ray said. 'Men won't part with the scrip, because each note is worth a dollar or more.'

'Well, let's hope, for all our sakes, that Worthington and my boss come to terms.'

'He'll need to provide actual cash up front for your bank to take scrip,' Partee pointed out.

'I'm sure Miss Hawthorn will work something out with him.'

'You're right, of course. She wouldn't have taken

over the bank unless she had a plan to convert the scrip to ready cash.'

Tazz downed the last of his drink and pushed away from the table. 'Well, I'm calling it a night.' He gave a nod to the man. 'Nice meeting you, Partee.' Then to Ray, 'and a pleasure hearing you sing, as always.'

'Thanks for the gratuity,' she replied, displaying a wide smile. 'You're the most generous man in the house tonight.'

'Ray!' her father bellowed. 'Don't sit around getting a fat behind! There's customers at the tables who need drinks!'

'Yeah, Pa,' she responded wearily. 'I'll check on them.'

'I'll be seeing you,' Tazz finished, leaving the two of them together. When he reached the door, he glanced back and noticed they were whispering back and forth intently. He hoped Partee wasn't jealous over his little donation or the flattering words from Ray. It was not his intention to come between the two lovers.

He was out into the cool night air, walking towards the boarding-house, when he spied the Worthington carriage. It was too dark to see who was driving, but it stopped to let Colena climb out. She said something to the driver, then the fancy black vehicle made a turn around and rolled up the street. It was quickly lost in the darkness.

Tazz wondered how the meeting had turned out, but Colena did not linger. She was inside the building before he arrived. He resigned himself to going to bed and trying to get some sleep. Funny thing, he hadn't been sleeping or eating good since meeting up with

Colena. He wondered if women were bad for a man's health. It sure seemed so.

Colena was eager to get started. She was already seated at the breakfast table when Tazz entered the room. She gave him a salutary nod. He responded with a 'good morning, Miss Hawthorn' and sat down next to Millie.

Breakfast was a quiet offering, with a morning prayer and very little chatter, except for some idle talk about the weather. As for Tazz, she noticed he was taciturn and unusually withdrawn. Consumed with a bubbling enthusiasm, Colena hated being surrounded by several other people. She wanted to jump in and tell Tazz her plans for expansion and other banking concerns. There were so many things that needed doing.

Colena rushed through the meal and hurried off to her room for a final look in the mirror and to grab her bag. She frowned at the tattered edges on her hat. The small quill of green and yellow feathers had faded and wilted with age until they looked as if they had been plucked from a dead buzzard. Partee had said her new hat might arrive as early as Saturday. She certainly hoped so. A lady of her position shouldn't be wearing anything so worn and decrepit about town.

With the hat neatly in place, she debated on whether she should wait for Tazz to join her on the walk to the bank. She decided it was best not to make a habit of something she might later regret.

However, she discovered the choice was not her own to make. Tazz was on the porch when she came out of the boarding-house. He touched the brim of his hat in a courteous gesture and displayed a polite smile.

'If it's all right with you, Miss Hawthorn, I'll escort you to the bank.'

'It isn't necessary,' she replied, 'but I have no objection.'

Rather than falling in at her side, Tazz offered his arm. Colena hesitated only a moment, then accepted his courtesy and they walked together. After a few steps, she cast a sidelong glance at him.

'Tell me, how did your evening go with the lady from the saloon?'

'I got the impression she wants to be rich and spoiled.'

'Doesn't everyone?'

'Not me,' he answered. 'I'd be satisfied to have a little house with a garden spot and a good woman at my side. She could make a home and help raise our children. I'd work hard and earn us a living.'

'What if this vice-president position doesn't work out? What will you do then?'

'I can always put on a badge and be a town sheriff or something. I know a little about cattle too, so I could work on a ranch or start up a small spread of my own.'

Colena was struck by the simple wants of the man. She had worked alongside her father since she was old enough to count. Her world had always been one of finances, of wants and needs, of money and material things. How strange to hear a man ask for nothing more from life than bare necessities.

'How about yourself, ma'am?'

She flinched at his calling her ma'am, but decided it was proper, due to their boss–employer relationship. She adequately hid the emotion as he added: 'Was your evening with the local baron a success?'

'I made some definite progress. Mr Worthington has a fortune stashed in different banks around the country. I presented a convincing argument for him to move enough here so we can exchange scrip. Once he complies, we will be able to handle loans and transactions for all kinds of new customers.'

'Partee, the man who runs the store, doesn't much care if we take away his banking business. I figure that's a plus for our side. If Worthington asks, he'll get no argument from him.'

'Yes, I have also spoken to Mr Partee. He was nice enough to dispatch an order to Denver to obtain me a new hat.'

Tazz rotated about and looked at her inquisitively.

'Word around town is the big he-bull, Worthington, is a lady's man – or thinks he is. You have any trouble with him?'

'He was a perfect gentleman throughout the evening.'

'So you didn't have to resort to using any of your wiles on him?'

She would have pulled away from him, had he not held her arm so tightly. Rather than make a scene, she gravitated a smile of beguilement.

'I'm sure he was interested, but I am quite able to be charming toward a man without contrivance.'

The frown which materialized on Tazz's face was evidence he didn't recognize the term. 'Was it that there *contrivance* we had in your office yesterday?'

The mention of their dalliance induced an instant ire. 'No! it certainly was not!'

'So was it maybe a *discussion*?'

Anger and shame battled for supremacy. A glut of heat rushed to flood color into her cheeks, but she remained mutinously composed. Calmly, she mustered up the words for her defense.

'Our ... *encounter*,' she used the word for want of a more appropriate term, 'was a simple demonstration of strength and independence. There was no feeling or emotion behind my behavior. I wanted you to appreciate that I am capable of competing on your level, Mr Spencer.'

'Oh, I sure enough *appreciated* it all right.'

'You know what I mean. It was a lesson in manners, an impersonal exhibit, not an invitation for a romantic union.'

'I sure felt something.'

'Think of it as akin to a sparring contest.' She became smug. 'Don't misconstrue my reaction as a passionate response.'

'Are you saying, was I to try it again, you would not respond?'

'I would respond, Mr Spencer,' she vowed, 'by slapping your face.'

'Why didn't you do that yesterday?'

She lifted her chin smugly. 'Because I had the feeling you expected it. I chose to defy your advance with an action equal to your own. The next time – should you be so foolish as to try – I shall not hesitate to dispense a clout up alongside your head!'

Tazz appeared tempted to put her words to the test, but they had reached the bank. He released his hold and Colena dug into her bag for the key. Tazz took it from her and opened the door to allow her to enter first. He followed her inside, pulled the door shut and locked it with the key. Then he handed the key back to Colena.

'You think maybe I ought to have a key myself, in case I ever need to open the bank or something?'

'I don't see why you would have need of it.'

'What if you're taken ill or want a day off?'

'I never take time off from work.'

'Seems to me, when I first met you at the river, you had been taking a swim whilst the bank was open in Denver.'

'There's a difference in situations now,' she clarified. 'That was my father's bank. This bank is my responsibility.'

'There's a dance at the livery Saturday night.' He changed the subject. 'How about we put in an appearance . . . for the sake of being sociable.'

'A dance?'

'You can dance, can't you?'

'Of course, I can dance. I—' she began.

'But you don't want to be seen with me,' he interrupted. 'Is that it?'

'I – I wouldn't wish for people to get the wrong idea.'

'Oh.' Tazz locked onto her with his eyes and gave a slight nod of his head. 'I can see how you might worry about it looking improper, ma'am.'

'I wasn't worried how—'

'But,' he cut her short again, 'I was only suggesting we be sociable. You wouldn't have to associate with me as if we were friends or anything more personal.'

She felt a sudden drop in her expectations.

'Besides,' he had not so much as paused for a breath, 'with you being so downright popular, I doubt there would be much of an opportunity for the two of us to kick up any straw together.'

'I don't know. We shouldn't—'

Tazz again did not let her reply. 'If you're ashamed of having me around, you don't have to allow me to escort you to the dance. I expect no one could latch onto the wrong idea, if we were careful and didn't let anyone see us speaking to one another.' His voice became smooth, the tone mocking. He had allowed her to jump to the wrong conclusion. Now he was toying with her. 'Fact is, I can pretend I never met you. If we bump into one another on the dance floor, I'll just say "excuse me, ma'am", and spin right off with my dancing-partner. If anyone asks, I'll tell them flat out I've never seen you before in my life.'

'All right, all right!' She put a stop to his exaggerations. 'I suppose I should put in an appearance . . . for the sake of the bank.'

He took a step towards her, placing himself so close that his body was nearly touching her own. It was an aggressive and impertinent position, yet she chose not to back away. She was not going to allow Tazz to intimidate her, not in her own bank!

'Then again,' he offered up a beguiling smile, 'if you change your mind about being seen in my company, I'd be right proud to accompany you to the dance.'

Colena was unable to reply, yet she experienced an involuntary shudder of delight at the proposal. She lowered her eyelids to hide the sensation from Tazz. If he were to realize how he affected her, he might be tempted to take advantage of the situation.

'I – I shall consider the offer, Mr Spencer.'

'I ain't never been around a woman who grabbed holt of my heart like you done,' he continued. 'From the moment I first heard your charming voice and peeked at them fancy pink bloomers, I knew you were something real special.'

'I . . .' She gulped down a fractious rise of emotion. 'I asked you not to use the word *ain't*. It isn't proper grammar for a vice-president.'

'Reckon my ignorance took a rear seat to my admiration, ma'am.'

Colena battled for sanity, attempting to recover from the shock of his candid confession.

'I've work to do,' she said quickly, seeking to escape his influence. 'I suppose you could accompany me to the dance as my escort.'

'Whatever you say.'

'And perhaps you are correct about becoming more familiar with the bank's daily operations,' she decided. 'Here,' she produced a slip of paper from her bag. 'It's the combination to the safe. You may have need of it, in case I am otherwise engaged. Memorize the numbers and then destroy the piece of paper.'

He looked down at the writing. 'Uh-huh, you trust me with the combination, but not a key to the door.'

'There is a second key in the safe. You may as well keep it with you, in the event there arises an emergency.'

Spencer gave an 'OK' response and Colena quickly fled to the refuge of her office. Once inside, she closed the door and gasped to catch her breath. Tazz was so much man . . . virile and charming! He seemed to have a magical hold over her. She needed some time alone . . . to think and regain control of her emotions and her sanity!

CHAPTER SEVEN

Saturday arrived and Tazz was looking forward to the dance. However, when he stopped by to see about escorting Colena to the dance, she was not at the boarding-house.

Millie told him a package had arrived for Colena at the store and she had gone to pick it up. An hour had passed since then. A check of her room was evidence she had been preparing to go to the dance. Tazz went by the store and spoke to Partee's aunt. She confirmed Colena had picked up a new hat and left.

Tazz searched for clues, but darkness quickly covered the land. He was tracing the path she would have taken, when he spied a shiny object on the ground at an alley. Kneeling down, he discovered it to be a button – one he recognized.

'Find something?' Kip Partee asked, having arrived to stand at his shoulder.

'I'm pretty sure this came from the sleeve of the dress Colena was wearing.'

'My aunt told me Miss Hawthorn picked up her hat. She said you came looking for her because she never returned to the boarding-house.'

'That's right,' Tazz answered.

Partee looked up the passage. 'You think someone grabbed her?'

Tazz moved a few inches. The ground was packed hard in the alley, as many of the locals used the path as a shortcut to reach the miners' housing outside of town. He continued to study each scuff mark and proceeded along the passage.

'Anything?' Partee wanted to know.

'This is where it happened all right. It appears she was snatched up and carried from this spot.' Tazz studied the markings for a few more moments. 'Miss Hawthorn wore distinctive shoes, but the prints stop here by the end of the alley.' He moved a few feet again, rose and shook his head. 'There were at least two men.'

'You can tell all that?' Partee was impressed. 'I don't see anything but a few smudges in the dirt.'

'If you check closely, you can make out where one of them stood at either side of the alley, waiting under in the shadows. By the shoe-prints, both were pretty fair-sized men. They left deep imprints, where the ground isn't packed down too hard.'

'Impressive deductions, Spencer. How do we go about finding them?'

'Only thing I can tell for sure is they aren't miners,' Tazz replied. 'The tracks show the sharp imprints of riding boots – deep heel-marks and narrow toes. These are custom-mades, not store-bought footgear.'

'So it's a couple of cowboys?'

'Not necessarily,' Tazz said. 'Could be guns for hire.'

'We can have a hundred men scouring the hills in twenty minutes.'

'All that would do is cause a panic and destroy what tracks there are. A bunch of men beating the woods would wipe out any chance of picking up their trail.'

'OK, Spencer, I see your logic there. What can I do to help?'

'I'd appreciate you rounding up a couple of trustworthy men, ones who know which end of a gun to point. If I locate these fellows, I might need some help.'

'I can ride with you if you want?'

Tazz arched his back, stiff from being stooped over for such a long time. 'I'll work it alone to start with and mark the trail. You can follow at first light.'

'Whatever you think is best,' Partee said. Then he offered: 'If you're going to start tracking, I'll pack you a sack of grub. It's the least I can do to help.'

'I appreciate it.'

'Meet you at the stable in what – fifteen minutes?'

'Should be about right, Partee. Thanks again.'

'You just find Miss Hawthorn, Spencer. We'll darn well get her back!'

Tazz waved a hand in agreement and Partee hurried off towards his store to put together some supplies. Tazz knew it would be extremely difficult to follow a trail in the dark, but he would use a lantern. Once he picked up the trail, he would stick to it.

Most fugitives only worried about concealing their trail for the first few miles. Then they became more concerned with speed and distance. Once they decided to stop worrying about hiding their tracks, he would be able to follow the kidnappers at a more rapid pace. He would spend the night on their trail and gain what distance he could. Whatever their motive for taking Colena, he wasn't going to give them any more time than possible to execute their plan.

Considering what their plan might be caused an icy fear to knot his stomach. Tazz mentally blocked the dread. He needed to remain objective to be of any real help to Colena. If he panicked, he wouldn't be able to do his job.

By afternoon the following day, Tazz was gaining ground more rapidly. Twice, during the night, he had been forced to follow a false trail, before discovering the men he pursued had back-tracked. They had also taken to a stream of water for nearly a mile. Again he had lost valuable time locating their exit. The men he followed had some savvy. If Tazz hadn't known the numerous tricks and been alert as to what to watch for, he would have lost them. As Tazz topped the crest of a hill, he paused to take a bearing on his position. In his head, he retraced the route.

The three had ridden from town, heading south, in the direction of Leadville, then they had turned to the west. From there, the trio had skirted a rugged mountain range and wandered back down as far as the Colorado river. Next, they wound a path to the north. It was clear they were not trying to escape from the country, only elude any pursuit.

He rested his horse, while considering the kidnappers' meandering route. He had visited some of the nearby ranchers and knew something of the lie of the land. In his estimation, the place where he now sat his horse was not more than ten or twelve miles from Penance.

104

'So you boys thought to lose a posse by riding a wide circle, huh?' he pondered aloud. Well, that trick might work to his favor. If they were holed up close by, it would be a simple matter to get help. Partee was likely only an hour or two behind him.

Off in the distance, he heard the snap of a branch or twig. He looked off in the distance, expecting it might be the small posse, but he didn't see anyone. During his ride, he had marked a clear trail for Partee and the others. He waited a full ten more minutes, just to be certain he was alone, then he began tracking again. With any luck, he would track down his prey before dark.

The two men didn't speak much, but Colena soon learned their names were Jigger and Mutt. Jigger was the more physically threatening of the pair, while Mutt watched her every move. She was frightened of Jigger, because he appeared to be a man who might hurt her. As for Mutt, she was more fearful of the growing interest she saw in his eyes.

They had ridden most of the night and eventually stopped at an old cabin. When daybreak came, the two kidnappers took turns. One remained inside the hovel with her and the other stayed outside keeping watch. For her bed, a dirty blanket was tossed into one corner. She attempted to sleep some, but her hands were bound behind her, which made it impossible to get comfortable. Also, she was concerned about what the two men intended. For the bulk of the day, Colena spent most of her time sitting with her back against the pine-slab wall, or trying to lie on her side and doze for a few minutes.

The two abductors were careful. Each time they traded positions, the man coming inside the cabin would check the cord about her wrists to see she was secure. Once satisfied she was helpless, that man would stretch out and try to get some sleep. There had been no morning or midday meal, but when late afternoon came, Mutt entered with an armload of firewood. He started a fresh fire before coming over to untie her.

'Time to get some chow cooking, woman,' he said, once she was free. 'There's beans, salt pork and some 'taters in the sack. Fix 'um up good and you get to eat.'

'Could I have a drink of water first?' she asked meekly. 'My throat is parched.'

'Yeah.' He grunted his OK. 'The canteen is next to the grub.'

Colena worked the cork out of the water container and tipped it up to take a few swallows. A bit of water spilled down her chin. When she paused to wipe it away, she subtly noticed the way Mutt's eyes had never left her. He stared longingly at her damp lips, then swept over her slender frame with a rudimentary regard, a gaze which caused a dirty feeling to creep along her flesh.

While the man waited and scrutinized her every move, she began the chore of fixing the meal. She found a pouch of salt and Mutt allowed her a small knife to peel and slice the potatoes. From the limited supplies available, it appeared their meals would be a staple of beans and strips of salt pork, along with hard rolls and coffee.

When the meal was ready, Mutt hailed Jigger from outside and he joined them inside the cabin for a few minutes. They ate in silence and Colena dared not ask questions. When she had finished her last bite of food, she began to wipe clean the dishes with a less than sanitary-looking cloth. She was about half-finished when something odd happened.

Mutt had been outside keeping watch. Suddenly, he hurried back inside to speak to Jigger. The two whispered back and forth for a few moments, as if discussing something important. Before Colena could complete her chores, she was quickly bound with rope and stuck into her corner. Then Mutt rushed back out the door.

'What's going on?' Colena risked the question. 'What's happening?'

'Just sit quiet,' Jigger told her. 'You'll find out when the time is right.'

Colena wondered why the two men were acting in such a bizarre fashion. Jigger took up a position at the only window of the cabin and kept watch. He stood there for a long time and the room began to grow dark with the setting of the sun. Finally, he went to the fireplace and added some wood. Once the flames sprang to life, he gave Colena a cruel smile and picked up the round box she had collected from Partee's store.

'Bought yourself a new bonnet, huh?'

She frowned at the remark. What was Jigger up to?

The man opened the box and removed the elegantly styled hat.

'Oh, yeah,' he said, 'I'll bet this cost you a few pennies.' When she remained silent, he scowled at her. 'What do you think?' He held it towards the fire. 'Should I toss it?'

107

Colena gasped. 'No, don't!'

He moved it nearer to the flames. 'Bet it would burn real good,' he taunted her.

'No! Please!' she pleaded with him. 'I've not even tried it on!'

'Did you say burn it?' he sneered. 'Is that what you're saying?'

'No!'

'You'll have to speak louder. I can't hear you.'

'Please!' she cried. 'Please don't!'

But he tossed the hat right into the fire.

'No. . .o. . .o. . .o!' Colena wailed, as the flames licked over the top of the beautiful hat and devoured it.

The door abruptly crashed open and slammed against the inside wall. Tazz burst through with his gun out! His eyes were wide and fearful. He covered Jigger and threw a quick look at Colena. His brows were drawn in an inquisitorial scowl.

'What did he do to you?' he demanded to know. 'Did he hurt you?'

Before Colena could reply, Mutt stepped in behind Tazz and shoved a gun muzzle into his back. 'Hold it, right there, Mr Hero,' he sneered.

Tazz had no chance. He slowly lifted his hands.

Jigger chuckled insolently and moved over to take Tazz's gun.

'Worked like a charm,' he said to Mutt. 'What a sap!'

Within a matter of seconds, Tazz was stripped of his gun and his wrists were bound behind him with rope. He was shoved down onto the blanket next to Colena, while Mutt and Jigger continued to laugh over the incident. Then they went out to find Tazz's horse and make sure he had come alone.

As soon as the two men were gone, Colena pivoted about to glare at Tazz.

'Of all the clumsy, bungled attempts! Is this your idea of a rescue?' She was angry and frustrated. Not only had her new hat been burned to ashes, but the effort to win her freedom had been completely botched. 'Where did you learn the art of liberating a captive? Didn't you stop to consider there might be two kidnappers!'

He groaned. 'I knew there were two of them. I've been following your trail for the last twenty-four hours. There were the distinct prints of three horses.'

'I don't believe it!' she continued to rant. 'You knew there were two kidnappers, yet you came rushing through the door like some maladroit novice. What manner of skulking tactic is that?'

He set his jaw and his voice became defensive. 'I was waiting for a chance to catch them off guard,' he explained. 'I had worked in close enough to get the drop on them the next time they changed guard duty.'

'So, why didn't you wait?' she demanded to know.

'I didn't think I had time.'

'Time!' she cried. 'They've had me in their meaty clutches all night and all day and you couldn't wait a few more minutes for them to change guard?'

'Yeah, that's right.'

'Why didn't you wait?' She again used a demanding tone of voice. 'What was your big hurry to rush in here and get captured?'

'I heard you cry out,' he retorted at last, displaying a trace of ire. 'It sounded like . . . I thought one of them was hurting you!'

Colena was stunned to a reflective silence. Jigger had been watching out the window, probably awaiting a signal from Mutt. He had purposely taunted her by destroying her new hat. She had lamented woefully and loudly over the loss. Tazz had heard her wail of distress and thought she was being attacked or injured. Sobering at the memory, she understood why he had risked his life by busting through the door – it had been to save her!

She swallowed her chagrin and annoyance by clearing her throat. 'Jigger tricked me into . . . crying out,' she admitted timorously. 'I had no idea you were close enough to hear me. I suppose some of the blame for your capture is mine.'

He made a short appraisal of her. 'I'm glad they didn't harm you.'

'No, I've not been mistreated.'

'When I heard you, it sounded as if you were in terrible pain. What did that low-down snake do? Threaten to cut you with a knife? Say he was going to beat you?'

'Not exactly.'

'Then what?'

'He used a dirty trick – all right?'

'What kind of trick?'

She sheepishly confessed. 'Jigger tossed my new hat into the fire.'

'Hat?' Tazz appeared confused.

'Yes, my brand-new hat!' She fumed. 'It only arrived from Denver yesterday. He burned it up in the fire! OK?'

A glimmer of understanding came into his eyes. 'Your hat,' he repeated. 'The guy forced you to cry out by setting fire to your hat.'

110

'Don't you dare belittle me, Tazz Spencer!' she scalded him angrily. 'If I recall, when I demanded you surrender your hat at the river, you were ready to die, rather than give it up. You do remember our first meeting?'

'I remember.'

'So don't give me a bad time about how agitated I sounded. I went to a lot of trouble to get that new hat.'

He allowed the matter to drop. 'Did they say why they grabbed you?'

'Didn't you find the message?' she asked. 'It was left under the bank door.'

He shrugged his shoulders. 'I never went inside the bank. Soon as you turned up missing, I set out following your tracks.'

'Then no one else knows I've been kidnapped?'

'Not to worry.' He was cynical. 'Doby will probably find the ransom letter when he arrives tomorrow and can't get inside the bank.'

'Oh, we're doing just great.'

He grew serious. 'Actually, Partee also knows about this. He is supposed to be following the markers I left for him and a posse.'

'And how are you supposed to signal him, while being tied up next to me?'

'Being a prisoner does make it a little more complicated.' Tazz stared at the door. 'I wonder how they knew I was out there watching?'

'One of them has been inside with me, but the other has been keeping vigil from outside. You obviously allowed the one on watch to see you.'

He took a deep breath and let it out slowly.

'I was too careful for that, lady. I've been in situations

111

like this before. I smelled smoke and left my horse a good way back in the hills. There's no way they could have seen me coming on foot.'

'How long had you been watching the cabin?'

'A few minutes. I was working my way close enough to make a move on them, when I heard you start to scream.'

'I didn't scream,' she contradicted him. 'I was merely voicing my objection to Jigger burning my hat.'

'Yeah, yeah, I know. Getting caught is my own fault.'

She paused in thought. 'Now that you mention it, something strange did take place earlier. I was in the middle of cleaning the dishes, after a meal, and they suddenly had me stop and tied me up.'

'How long ago was that?'

'Quite a while. Maybe as much as an hour.'

Tazz pondered the information. 'It makes no sense. I was still a half-mile away an hour ago. They couldn't possibly have known I was coming.'

'What does it mean?'

'I don't know. I'll ponder it some, soon as we're out of this fix.'

'And how do we escape our present predicament?'

'I've been in a few tight spots before. As they didn't kill me right off, it gives us time to figure something out. Don't you worry. These fellows are as good as in jail.'

'Maybe I should warn them as to how much trouble they're in.'

He grinned. 'We don't want them getting their guard up. Let them stay confident until I make my move and arrest them both.'

'I do so admire an optimist.'

'What's one of them eye-doctor types got to do with our situation?'

She groaned. 'I hope you don't get us both killed.'

The evening wore on and Jigger kept a pot of coffee on the fire. A couple hours after full dark, Mutt came in from being on watch. Jigger put on a jacket, poured himself a cup of brew and went out into the night. Mutt took a moment to check and see Tazz and Colena were both bound securely. Once satisfied, he paused to study Colena for a long moment.

'You thirsty?' he asked her.

'Yes, please.' She was appropriately meek.

Mutt retrieved his canteen, popped the cap and gave her a few sips. She thanked him when she had finished. He didn't offer any water to Tazz, so he didn't ask for any. Tazz didn't miss the glowing desire within his piggish eyes.

'You do as you're told,' Mutt spoke to Colena, 'and you won't get hurt none. We're in this for the money and nothing else. We don't aim to do you no harm.'

'What about Mr Spencer?'

He snorted. 'Him neither, if he don't get cute. We only want the money.' Mutt then rolled out his blanket and prepared to get some sleep.

Colena attempted to lie down on her side, but it was awkward having her head tilted at such an angle. Mutt secretly watched her every move as she shifted her position.

Tazz was stretched out, lying on one shoulder. His hands were securely bound, but there were no bonds to

113

cramp his mind. Mutt's attraction for the girl was obvious. He had shown concern for her by offering her water, all the while ogling her. A man blinded by infatuation had the tendency to get careless. It gave Tazz an idea.

He waited and watched for a few minutes. Mutt finally lay back and relaxed on his blankets. When he closed his eyes, Tazz nudged Colena and lifted his head enough to get her attention. With a wink, he used his foot to lift the hem of her skirt and push it higher up on her leg.

Colena bore into him with a curious frown, trying to decide what he was up to.

Tazz waited a few seconds, continuing to keep a sharp eye on Mutt. Then he lifted his leg and used the toe of his boot to shove the material of Colena's dress upward again. The action exposed her pink bloomers nearly to her waist and brought a gasp from her lips.

'What do you think you are doing?' Colena whispered anxiously.

'Shush!' he whispered back. 'Play along!'

'What's going on over there?' Mutt sat up, instantly alert. 'I hear the whispering betwixt you two.'

Tazz rolled over, lying with his hands under the small of his back. He lifted his head and gave a nod at Colena.

'It's the lady,' Tazz explained. 'She was trying to get comfortable and got her skirt twisted and hiked up around her waist. I told her I wasn't about to use my teeth and pull it back down, just so's she could keep her modesty.'

Mutt came to his knees and turned up the lamp. He

stared hungrily at Colena, practically licking his lips at the sight. Finally, he cleared his throat.

'Yeah, well, I guess I can help with that.'

'Would you please?' Colena took her cue at the situation. 'I was trying to manage a suitable position for sleeping and my skirt became wadded up. It's not only the embarrassment, but I know it will be chilly before morning.'

Mutt came to hunker down over Colena. Instead of pulling the dress down into place at once, he paused for a moment, allowing his gaze to rest on her pink bloomers. It was such an enticing view, he was unable to look away.

'I suspected you were a gentleman,' Colena spoke calmly, while her face glowed red from the humility of revealing her wares so wantonly.

Mutt reached for the hem of her skirt, where it was balled up at her waist . . . .

Tazz struck without warning, kicking like a spooked stallion! With Mutt's eyes completely focused on the satin bloomers, he was blind-sided. The sole of the boot caught him right in the throat!

Mutt was driven back onto his heels from the force of the blow. His hands flew up to his damaged windpipe. Before he could regain his senses, Tazz sprang to his feet. He drove a shoulder into the man and knocked him onto his back.

Gasping for air, helpless to fight back, Mutt's jaw was an easy target for Tazz's boot. He kicked him unconscious with one solid shot.

'Hurry!' he ordered Colena. 'Turn around with your back to me.'

115

Even as she was getting to her knees and doing as he instructed, Tazz removed a knife from a sheath on Mutt's belt. He backed up to Colena and pushed the knife handle into her hands.

'Hold it still!' he ordered, frantic to free his hands.

She kept the blade facing out, gripped tightly. Tazz put his tied wrists up against the knife and rubbed in an up and downward motion until the edge cut through the rope. Then he peeled off the remaining cord and retrieved his gun. He was none too quick.

Jigger must have heard the commotion. He rushed through the door with pistol in hand. He spied Mutt lying on the floor and turned the gun towards Tazz.

The blast shattered the stillness of the night and resounded within the closed-in walls. But it was not Jigger's gun which had fired. The smoking gun belonged to Tazz. Jigger was struck in the chest and the force of the bullet knocked him back out the door. Tazz followed quickly, but it wasn't necessary. The man wasn't going anywhere. He was dead before he crumbled to the ground.

Tazz returned inside the cabin, took a moment to tie Mutt's hands behind him, then took the knife Colena was still holding and cut the rope which had bound her. She was shaking from the sudden trauma and whirled about right into his arms.

'Oh, Tazz!' she murmured breathlessly, hugging him close. She placed her cheek up next to his own, with her eyes closed tightly. 'That was frighteningly close!'

He pushed back from her and smiled. 'We make a good team.'

'We could have been killed!' she retorted. 'If you had

been one second slower getting loose, if you had stopped to untie me first, if your kick had not disabled Mutt, if you hadn't fired first . . . Those are a lot of ifs!'

Rather than argue, Tazz kissed her lightly on the lips. Colena returned a slight pressure of her own in surrender. Tazz held the kiss for several exhilarating seconds, before he eventually broke contact. Colena expelled a rush of air, as if startled at having been holding her breath.

Tazz looked at her and noticed how the lamp's flickering light reflected in her eyes like a shower of sparks.

'I'll be hanged if you ain't the most special lady I ever met,' he said warmly. 'Was that there a thank you kiss, or are we maybe going to be more than a bank president and vice-president?'

Colena appeared to recover her wits and removed herself from his grasp. With a renewed composure, she spoke with a subtle calmness.

'You were correct on your first assessment of the situation, Mr Spencer. I wished to thank you for rescuing me.'

'We'd best get organized. Partee should be coming with a posse. Like I told you before, he is supposed to be right behind me.'

Even as the words were spoken, there was the sound of several horses coming into the yard. Tazz and Colena went out to meet the small posse. Partee, Boyle and Peters rode up to the cabin and stopped next to Jigger's body.

'You got her!' Partee stated the obvious. Then he looked at the man on the ground. 'Killed one of the kidnappers, too.'

'The other one is inside. He'll live long enough to hang.'

Partee gave a tilt of his head to the other two men.

'Let's round up their horses and load the body. We'll get started as soon as we're ready to ride.'

'We going to head back in the dark?' Boyle asked.

'It isn't more than a two-hour ride,' Partee told him. 'I'd judge we ain't more than a mile or so from the main trail. We can make good time once we hit the road.'

'Thought you might catch up sooner.' Tazz spoke to the storekeeper.

'Would have, if we hadn't lost you at the creek.' Partee gave a heave of his shoulders. 'What can I say, we ain't much good at tracking – even with you leaving a plain trail to follow. If we hadn't heard the gunshot, we'd have been camped out there in the woods and waited for daylight.'

'Anyone find the note at the bank?'

'Boyle brought it over to the store, just before we were getting ready to ride out. These two kidnappers were asking for ten thousand dollars.'

'We didn't have more than a couple hundred in the bank.' Colena spoke up. 'How did they expect anyone to pay the ransom?'

'I guess they figured your father would send the money,' Partee replied. 'The note said the bank had a week to come up with the money.'

'Your dad could have sent the money by coach and it would have been here in time,' Tazz said. 'That must have been their idea.'

'We can ask the second abductor,' Partee suggested.

'You say he's still alive?'

'I dimmed his lamps some, but he should be OK.'

Even as the words were spoken, Boyle herded Mutt out the door. The man's hands were still tied securely. He glanced at his fallen comrade and glared at Tazz.

'We should have kilt you right off, when we first caught you. Any man who could follow what little trail we left – you had to be trouble.'

'I'm sorry I had to kill your friend. There wasn't time to try and only wound him.'

'You best hope I don't never get loose, mister. Jigger was my cousin. I get the chance, I'll pay you back for killing him.'

'You won't get that chance!' Partee shot back. 'Put him on a horse, Boyle. We'll wire the circuit judge and hold a quick trial for our dirty friend. I doubt he'll be so tough after twenty years of busting rocks in a territorial prison!'

'Come on, tough guy.' Boyle gave a yank on his arm, dragging him towards the picket line of horses. Peters was already there, busy saddling the animals so they could get started for Penance.

'Did I hear right? Did that guy say they had caught you, Spencer?' Partee wanted to know. 'How did you manage to get loose and turn the tables on them?'

'With a bit of luck and a pair of fancy bloomers.'

Partee frowned. 'Say what?'

'Never mind!' Colena interjected sharply. 'Let's get going. I'm tired and sore from this whole affair. I want a bath and some sleep before I have to go back to work at the bank.'

'Whatever you say,' Partee acquiesced. 'I'll lend the boys a hand.'

As he hurried over to help with the horses, Colena pivoted to face Tazz.

'What's the idea of telling him about exposing my . . . my unmentionables!'

Tazz hoisted his eyebrows in total innocence. 'I only reported what happened.'

'No one is in need of that much detail!' she rasped. 'I don't want everyone in town to know how I wantonly displayed my . . .' she sought the word, 'my wares!'

'Actually, I reckon it was me who done displayed your wares,' Tazz corrected, exhibiting a smirk. 'I seen the way that Mutt fella was drooling at the chops over you. I figured it would only take a peek at your satin undertrousers to catch him off guard.'

'Yes, I grasped your logic, Mr Spencer. But I would prefer our method of subterfuge not become common knowledge. Do you understand me?'

'Sure 'nuff,' he said, exhibiting a half-smile. 'I'll leave the telling of the story to you. I'm sure you can *skirt* the truth without commencing to make *blooming* lies about the facts.'

At Colena's annoyed frown, he continued the cocky simper. 'Besides which, getting a second look at them pretty lace bloomers of yours ought to remain a private matter between the two of us.'

'You are an insufferable rake, Mr Spencer.'

'Ain't a rake something pulled back of a team of horses to gather hay into a row?'

'All right! how about Lothario, lecher, rascal, scoundrel!' she stated hotly. 'Do you recognize any of those titles?'

'Not so much,' he said smoothly. 'Maybe it will

120

become clear when you get to more favorable type words like lover, beau or sweetheart.'

Colena threw up her hands in exasperation and spun away from him. She marched over to the string of horses and snatched hold of the reins of one of them. Without waiting for anyone to lend a hand, she raised her foot into the stirrup, grabbed hold of the pommel and pulled herself up into the saddle.

'Let's get started!' She barked the order at Partee.

'We're almost ready,' he explained hastily. 'Only have to load up the body of the dead kidnapper and we're on our way.'

'So cease the banal dialogue and tend to the chore!' Colena snapped.

Within minutes the small troop was moving through the brush. Once they reached the beaten trail, the horses made good time. As Partee had predicted, it was not yet midnight when they reached the outskirts of Penance.

A short way from the boarding-house, Tazz reined his horse over next to Colena.

'To avoid being mobbed and answering a lot of questions, mayhaps you ought to slip away at Millie's place,' he suggested. 'I'll see to your horse, and me and the others can take care of Mutt and see to Jigger's body.'

'Thank you, Mr Spencer. I appreciate your concern for my welfare.'

'I would like to say one more thing, before we part company.'

'And what is that?'

Tazz turned in the saddle to look at her. 'About kissing you and all back there at the cabin. I don't believe

121

it was only you thanking me.' He paused, piercing the darkness with his intense gaze.

'Oh, you don't.' There was a warning ring to her voice. 'And what, precisely, do you think it was, Mr Spencer?'

'Let's just say, I'd admire to be more than friends with you, ma'am.'

Colena maintained an outward equanimity.

'I haven't slept in two days, and I'm tender and ache all over from riding for such a long period. Perchance we could discuss this at a more opportune time.'

'Is it that I'm not city-slicker and educated enough for you?'

'As I indicated, this isn't the time or place for invoking a deliberation on the subject. I owe you a debt for saving me from those kidnappers. You risked your life to help me, so I am bound to feel a certain amount of gratitude.'

'I don't want your gratitude.'

'Then you'll have to allow me time to sort out my feelings. I don't wish to make any allegation concerning our association at the moment.'

He sighed. 'Sure, whatever that there allegation thing is, Miss Hawthorn. Take all the time you need. I got nothing but time . . . leastways, for the next three months.'

CHAPTER EIGHT

True to his promise, Tazz gave Colena a wide berth the next few days. He was cordial, walked her to the bank from the boarding-house and sometimes escorted her home after work. However, he made no mention of their previous conversation. Friday morning, Harcore Worthington entered the bank.

'Good morning, Mr Spencer,' he greeted Tazz. 'I've come to speak with Miss Hawthorn.'

Tazz gave him a nod, then led the way to Colena's office. He knocked once, then opened the door.

'Mr Worthington to see you, boss,' Tazz told her, moving aside to allow the man to enter. Then, once he was in the room, he said: 'I'll close the door for your privacy.'

Colena smiled and tipped her head in a nod of approval.

Tazz gave the man a short once-over. It was a male appraisal, the kind of succinct evaluation a suitor often gave a rival. Worthington ignored the look, waiting to be left alone with Colena before speaking.

Tazz closed the door and returned to his desk. Thirty

minutes passed before Worthington appeared at the exit.

'Good day, Harcore,' Tazz heard Colena's cheerful voice. 'And thank you again!'

Worthington strode importantly past Tazz and went out of the bank. As soon as he was gone, Colena waved to Tazz, signaling him to come to her office.

He had hardly entered the room and she closed the door. 'I did it!' she cried, throwing her arms around his neck. Overjoyed with jubilance, she kissed him flush on the mouth.

Tazz responded at once, using his strong arms to lift her right off her feet. He turned completely around with her, before setting her back down. She pushed away at once, unable to hold back the important news.

'Worthington is going to put ten thousand dollars into my bank!' Colena gasped, bubbling over with a barely contained enthusiasm. 'I've done it, Tazz!' She was ecstatic. 'I've done it!'

He smiled at her excitement. 'I'm happy for you. I know this will help the bank.'

'Oh, yes! yes! A chance to prove my worth to my father. It's what I've wanted ever since I learned to walk. With the scrip exchangeable for cash, Penance is going to become a real town . . . and my bank will be a part of it. You'll see!'

His eyes were steady, evaluating her, assessing the significance of this event, while keeping a firm control on his own desires. Colena noticed a number of unanswered questions in his gaze.

'What?' she asked.

'I was about to ask the same thing,' he said guardedly. 'What about us?' Without allowing her to escape his scrutiny, he added: 'That is, supposing there is an us?'

'There will be ample time for sorting out our relationship later, Tazz,' Colena said quickly. 'I mean, there is so much to do, so many changes coming to Penance. I've got to make plans for expansion and speak to Tolken about advertising. Once the money arrives, I need to spread word that the bank is ready to exchange scrip. There will be business loans to offer, ranch payrolls to acquire, transfers of money from the railroad – a thousand things to do!'

A coolness seeped into his demeanor and he released her from his arms. Oddly, she appeared uncomfortable over the dismissal.

'I reckon you answered my question.'

'For heaven's sake, Tazz!' She displayed an impatience. 'Don't you understand? I've worked for years to prove I could make a go of a business on my own. I'll show my father that I'm every bit as capable as my brother. It's all I've ever wanted. I can't forgo my life-long dream by getting all starry-eyed over some hulking, gun-toting, ex-deputy!'

'Enough said.' He backed up another step. 'I just wanted to know where I stood.'

'Tazz, please . . .'

'You don't have to hit me over the head with a dumb stick. I get the idea.'

'Can't you understand? I have to do this!'

'Yeah, I see that I can play second fiddle or quit the band.'

She frowned. 'Stop acting like a spoiled child who

125

can't have his way! You should be happy for me! I'm on the verge of making this bank a success. It's my chance to show my father I can do the job.'

'Maybe you should take time to listen to yourself, ma'am,' he drawled. 'Every word out of your mouth is me or my or I'm going to do this or that. Not once have you mentioned a we or our in your fancy vocabulary.'

She clenched her teeth tightly. 'That's because I'm the one responsible for the bank, Tazz! We both know you're not really a vice-president! Father sent you to be a watchdog, not to handle any actual banking business.'

Tazz flinched from the stinging indictment. Truth or not, her directness was another blow to his pride.

'I signed on for three months . . . and I'm a man of my word.' Then opening the door, 'But, just so there's no misunderstanding, I won't be staying one day longer. Feel free to line yourself up a real vice-president, one who will fawn and bow to your every whim, without strings or conditions!' With the words hanging in the air, he left the room, crossed to the front entrance and left the bank.

All manner of emotions were at war inside Colena. Part of her wanted to cuss out the man's stubborn, narrow-mindedness, while the remainder of her wanted to cry out in agony at having him walk out on her. What was the matter with him? Didn't he know she wanted him to be a part of her accomplishments, that he should be steadfast and supporting of her success? Why couldn't he get it through his thick head?

There were no customers at the teller window so Doby approached the office. When Colena took notice of him, he gave a tip of his head toward Tazz's vacant desk.

'There is a client waiting to speak to Mr Spencer. Do you know if he will be back before closing, Miss Hawthorn?'

'It's Friday.' She excused Tazz'z departure. 'I allowed he could leave early.'

'The lady came in right after you summoned Tazz to your office. She said she wanted to speak to him about investing some money.'

Colena recognized the female entertainer from the Open Pit saloon, ReAnn Gannon, sitting in a chair next to Tazz's desk. She uttered a sigh.

'I'll see to it.'

'Very good, ma'am,' said Doby, and returned to his position at the teller window.

At Colena's approach, the woman glanced up. A cool appraisal seeped into her painted face and puckered lips.

'Can I help you, Miss Gannon?' Colena asked.

'I prefer to do my business with a man,' ReAnn replied curtly. 'No offense.'

'I'm the bank president.' Colena stated the obvious. 'If you wish a consultation with someone about finances, I am the most qualified person within a hundred miles.'

'I'll grant you must have something going for you,' ReAnn said, looking Colena over from head to foot with a careful inspection. 'After all, you've got Worthington panting at your heels.'

'You know Mr Worthington personally, do you?'

'We were . . . sociable for a time,' ReAnn admitted,

'but then I found out he ain't the marrying kind.' With a shrug of her shoulders she added: 'I'm not one to dangle on a string for no man – even a rich, he-bull like him.'

'On that point, we are in perfect agreement.'

ReAnn cast a patently judgemental look at the door, as if deciphering the reason Tazz had left the bank. A knowing look came into her moderately attractive face.

'However, Miss Banker,' she said, 'I would have a complete change of heart for the right man. If I really loved him, and if he was willing to marry me proper, I'd give him so much love and affection, he would be the one dangling on *my* string.'

Colena felt a crimson flush come into her cheeks. She could do absolutely nothing to hide the warmth, so she quickly changed the subject.

'If you prefer to discuss your situation with Mr Spencer, I'm sure he will be available on Monday.'

ReAnn used a taunting tone of voice. 'Perhaps I'll see him before then.' With a sly simper, 'If there's one thing I do know, it's how to console a man.'

Colena grated her teeth together. 'I'm sure your comforting demeanor comes from a great deal of experience.'

ReAnn rose to her feet, cast a last, canny simper at Colena, then swayed across the room and out the door. She didn't bother to say goodbye or add anything to their conversation. It wasn't necessary. They understood one another perfectly!

Tazz didn't feel like sitting across from Colena at the dinner table. He wandered over to the Open Pit. Not yet hungry, he decided to have a drink and maybe sit in at a card-game. Boyle was alone at a table playing solitaire, so he ordered a beer and joined him.

'You winning?' he asked.

'Not even when I cheat,' the man grumbled

'Where's your partner?'

'His turn at the smokehouse,' Boyle answered, 'watching our prisoner.'

'Any word yet on when to expect the circuit judge?'

'Partee sent off a wire, but the judge won't be through for at least another week. Then we'll still have to keep an eye on the prisoner till a marshal comes to pick him up.' He paused. 'That is, if he gets prison time and not the noose. I reckon we can hang him, if the judge decides the charge is severe enough to warrant it.'

'To his credit, he didn't hurt the lady.'

'Yeah, there's something to be said for that.'

'I don't believe I ever thanked you and Peters for coming to lend a hand after the kidnapping. If Jigger had been the one to get off the first shot, you boys would have had to save the lady banker.'

'You're sure welcome, Spencer, but save your thanks for Partee. He's the one who brung me and Peters along.' He chuckled. 'O'course, I got to figure he was looking to make himself out to be the hero.'

'How so?'

Boyle continued: 'He had me and Peters hang back and give him a couple hours to locate you and the girl on his own. I'm thinkin' he was of a mind to rescue her or help you all by himself. Probably figured it would make a big impression on Worthington. I swear, he's got it in his head to become a partner or something. He left us sitting in the shade, while he went off wandering through the hills, trying to catch up with you.'

'Then you weren't lost, like he said?'

'Nope, only biding our time while he located either the hideout or you and come back for us. It didn't work out, 'cause he lost your tracks. By the time we managed to pick up your trail again, it was too dark to reach the shack. It's lucky we happened to be close enough to hear the gunshot from when you killed that Jigger fellow.'

Tazz stored the information, while continuing the small talk. 'I had a little luck on my side. A second or two difference and I'd be the one buried six feet underground.'

'It worked out OK. We got the lady back safe and sound.'

'Yes, we did, and I still owe you a drink.'

'No harm in that.' He flashed a wide grin. 'No harm atall.'

Tazz ordered a drink for Boyle and then they played some Casino. The small talk between them was commonplace, simply to pass the time, but Tazz continued to mull over what Boyle had told him.

Mutt and Jigger must have known Colena's father had another two banks, so they had expected him to put up the money for the ransom. However, they also had to know their plan meant keeping her hostage for several days, until money could be sent from Denver. With Tazz left behind to form an all-out search, he wondered how they could have hoped to stay at their chosen hideout for an entire week without being discovered.

Of course, he could only speculate. The two men might have been intending to keep moving around every few days. Mutt had become mute after his capture. He would likely go to prison or the gallows without ever explaining their plan.

Concerning Partee, Boyle probably had it straight. If the storekeeper had impressed Worthington with a single-handed rescue, it could have added some clout to his position. He had been with Worthington since the construction of the company store, so he might have been looking to earn some kind of promotion or get himself a bonus. That angle made sense, especially with Partee trying to win Ray's hand in marriage.

He remembered how Ray had told him she wanted the finer things life had to offer – a house in the city, money for clothes, a chance to rub shoulders among the élite. She didn't sound eager to tie herself to a simple storekeeper. She wanted to leave Penance and start a new life. A simple raise in Partee's pay would not be sufficient. Possibly, Partee had hoped to earn a substantial amount from the rescue – a reward from Colena's father.

The puzzle was like stirring the water in a puddle to see more clearly. The end result only made the water more cloudy from disturbing the muddy bottom.

Saturday afternoon, Colena was busy writing a letter to her father, when a tap came at her door. She was surprised to see Kip Partee at her door. He was holding a box in his hand – a round box.

'Stage arrived a few minutes ago,' he said, presenting

the package to her. 'I decided not to take a chance and to deliver this personally.'

Colena took the box and placed it on the small writing-table. She popped the lid to discover a charming dress hat, complete with a small spray of brightly colored yellow and green feathers.

'How did you . . . ?' She removed the hat and immediately stepped over in front of the mirror to try it on. 'I didn't know you had ordered me a replacement hat. I forgot to even ask you about it.'

'I took it on my own initiative,' he said. 'And this one is free of charge.'

'No!' she exclaimed. 'I couldn't do that!'

Partee shook his head. 'Yes, Miss Hawthorn. I feel responsible for your being grabbed last Saturday night. If I had thought to send the hat over with the runner, there would have been no way those two men could have snatched you at the alley.'

'It wasn't your fault.'

'None the less, I want you to have this one gratis.'

'If you insist – but it isn't necessary.'

Partee surveyed her for a lengthy moment. 'It looks great on you.'

'It's a beautiful hat.'

'Wish I'd have thought to order one for Ray.'

Colena replied with, 'Oh?' and he emitted a sigh.

'She wants to be a proper lady. You know, one who is fussed over and treated special.'

'All women want that.'

He still appeared downhearted. 'Yeah, but I don't know when I'll be able to afford everything she wants.'

'Money shouldn't be a girl's only guiding factor.'

'I ought to have learned to live with the idea by now. Material things are real important to Ray.' He ducked his head and grated his teeth. 'Shortly after her father started up the Open Pit saloon, Ray tried to win the heart of Worthington.' The pain and disgust was reflected in his voice. 'She went after him with a vengeance.'

'She mentioned she had been friends with him at one time.'

'Friends!' He growled at the bitter memory. 'It took her several months to discover he isn't the marrying kind. Once she realized he only wanted her company, so he could enjoy her favors, she broke off their relationship.'

'I suppose her motives are understandable. I've heard how she has been forced to entertain and wait on miners since she learned to walk and talk.'

'That's the truth all right. Her father used her as a stepping-stone to get where he is today. She's been his personal slave all these years. Sixteen hour days, serving meals or drinks to rowdy miners, then having to sing and dance to bring in customers. She's had a hard road.'

'Perhaps she'll decide being a wife is enough one day.'

His shoulders sagged. 'I wish I could believe that, but it don't seem so. Take her latest personal goal, for instance. I think she has set her cap for your vice-president. I guess she figures he is going to be a bank manager himself one day.'

It was as if a rush of cold, inert air had entered Colena's lungs and been absorbed into her chest cavity.

133

She recalled the woman's combative manner at the bank and experienced an immediate pang of jealousy.

She spoke carefully, withholding her emotions. 'Mr Spencer is quite personable, but he has a great deal to learn about banking. I don't expect him to be appointed to a manager position for a long while.'

'It must not make any difference to Ray. She and Spencer are getting real cozy over at the saloon. They've spent some time together lately and Ray told me not to bother her tonight. I think they are planning something special. I tell you, Miss Hawthorn, it's about to eat me alive inside.'

'I was under the impression you and Ray were sort of engaged?'

'There never was a ring or formal announcement made,' he explained. 'I thought we had an understanding between us.' He gnashed his teeth. 'Guess I was wrong.'

'I'm sorry.'

'Yeah, well, I won't give up without a fight. That's why I should have ordered a second hat or something.'

'If you wish, you can present this one to her. I can wait until . . .'

He shook his head. 'No, ma'am, but I thank you for the offer. Truth is, Ray prefers them bigger hats, the kind with wide brims and a whole lot more plumage. She likes people to notice her.'

'I understand.' Colena put on a sympathetic mien. 'But I still feel I should pay you for the hat.'

'No way, ma'am.' Partee uttered a sour grunt. 'But it's a gift from me, not Worthington. He don't own me – not a hundred per cent anyway.'

'The way he owns this town, I'm somewhat surprised he ever agreed to allow a bank to assume operation.'

'We don't make many loans,' Partee told her. 'After all, who can afford to pay five or six per cent interest every month?'

'That's pretty steep all right.'

'It wouldn't be so bad, if he wasn't cutting the throats of the miners to start with. Did you know he pays some of them two dollars and fifty cents a day?' Partee was growing more irate with every word. 'Any other mine, any other place in the country is paying three dollars or more. He can get away with it because he scours the jails and prisons for men who are debtors or convicted of minor crimes.'

'Criminals can't expect the best jobs.' Colena attempted some justification.

'I've talked to these boys, ma'am. Some of them were only involved in a fist-fight or arrested for a minor offense. There ain't no killers or bandits in the lot. And a good many were just broke or couldn't pay the loan interest at some crooked bank.' He paused. 'No offense.'

'I'm aware that there are many unscrupulous banks across the country.'

'Yeah, well, these guys deserve a chance to get even. You've seen them at the Sunday meeting. Some are family men, with a wife and kids to support – yet we charge them twice what things should cost, and then Worthington cheats them on their wages.'

'How about you?' she asked. 'He must treat you better than the miners?'

'I earn a salary and a small percentage for having

135

built the store from scratch. It seemed like a good deal on paper, until you consider I have to tend the store six days a week, do Worthington's books and run his scrip operation. My aunt works sixty hours a week helping me in the store, and I spend at least that many hours there too. It sure didn't take long for me to discover the money I earn is less than if I had gone to work in the mines. I would up and quit, but I've got too much invested in the business.'

'Maybe you could sell?'

'Worthington allowed me some operating credit when I began to stock goods and supplies.' Partee sighed. 'I ended up owing him more money than I had to start with. I have to keep working just to break even.'

'Perhaps you can get a loan from my bank and pay him off. The deposit from Worthington is due in tomorrow. Once we have the capital on hand, I'll have funds available at a reasonable interest rate.'

He smiled at her offer. 'I'd like that. How about I buy you dinner at the Open Pit tonight? I could bring along my books and show you the numbers.'

Colena hesitated. She didn't like the idea of being seen publicly with a man who was supposed to be engaged. None the less, it was a business function. She was a bank president, and as such, this sort of dinner was sometimes necessary.

'You could wear your new hat,' Partee suggested. 'The food is quite good and I happen to know there was a delivery today from an orchard over on the Western Slope. They will be offering peach pie.'

That bit of news convinced Colena. She loved fresh peaches. 'If you'll give me a few minutes, I'll put on something more appropriate.'

'Good!' Partee said, displaying a wide smile. 'Good! I'll run over and pick up my account book and be waiting on the porch for you.'

'I'll be along as soon as I am presentable.'

Partee left and Colena changed into a pleasant gown of gossamer over satin. It was a little dressy for the occasion, but she needed something to equal the decorative new hat. Next, she put a bit of paint on her lips and applied a light rouge to her cheeks. She brushed her hair, then pinned it in place so the hat would seat attractively on her head.

In introspect, she suddenly wished this was to be an evening spent with Tazz, a quiet meal, a walk in the evening dusk, perhaps a goodnight kiss. A quick shake of her head removed the notion. She had to stick to business, and the dinner was part of being a bank manager.

Ray made a point of informing Tazz about the arrival of fresh peaches. It was all the convincing he needed to have his evening meal at the Open Pit. There were a number of other customers eating there this night, most of whom knew about the special dessert.

Ray was not working alone at the café side. A daughter of one of the miners was also helping serve meals. After the main course, when it came time for the promised dessert, Tazz was surprised by Ray bringing out two plates of pie. She smiled warmly and sat down next to him.

'I haven't had time for more than a taste yet,' she explained to Tazz.

137

'Looks and smells great,' he said, as he picked up a fork. 'Been a spell since I had me some peach pie.'

'Ummm,' Ray said, savoring the flavor from her first bite. 'Durned if it isn't sweeter than most of the men I've kissed.'

Tazz also relished his bite of the fresh peach pie. 'Sweet and juicy,' he agreed, 'but no dessert is a match for the right woman's kiss.'

Ray laughed. 'Why, Tazz, you are a poet!'

He arched his brows. 'The words didn't even rhyme.'

'Making the words rhyme doesn't make one a poet,' she told him. 'A poet can be anyone who has feeling and is compassionate; he's a person who sees purpose, rather than mere oil-paint on a picture.'

'You don't say?'

She produced a charming laugh, while her eyes sparkled. 'A poet looks at the stir of the wind and thinks of the glory of heavens, not the swirling dust before his eyes.'

'I expect there's often more to be seen than what meets the eye,' Tazz attempted to be philosophical, 'I reckon that's what you're talking about.'

Ray's eyes seemed to flick away for an instant, but she quickly reverted her attention to Tazz and leaned closer. A seductive smile curled her lips, while her long lashes fluttered slightly.

'I'm talking about a man who sees a woman as more than a servant, one who feels driven to give the world to the love of his life.'

Before he realized her intention, Ray leaned across the table and touched his lips with her own. He was surprised enough not to think of pulling away. He

138

simply sat there, dumbfounded at the unexpected action.

'Ummm,' Ray cooed softly, pulling back to smile again. 'You're right about a kiss. When it's from the right man's lips, it is better than the peach pie.'

Tazz felt a rush of embarrassment and wondered at the gal's sudden show of affection. He was searching his brain for something appropriate to say, when he felt a burning probe at the back of his head. He rotated around to discover the sensation was derived from the daggers of Colena's white-hot glare!

He instantly sat back in his chair, while Ray nonchalantly returned to eating her dessert. She continued to smile at him, but it was obvious the little scene had not happened by accident.

'Why'd you kiss me just now?' he asked her, straightforward.

'I wanted to compare you against the peach pie.' Ray was quick with both her reply and her innocent yet beguiling simper. 'I wanted proof of your point.'

'You're not concerned that Partee walked in and seen us?'

She glanced the storekeeper's direction, but her expression didn't change.

'Kip and I are at odds right now. He wants me to marry him and go to work in his store.' She shrugged a shoulder. 'Why should I change one job for another? I want more than to raise a flock of kids and work myself to death.'

'Love ought to count for something,' he argued.

'I've been a slave all my life,' she replied harshly. 'Bend, serve, entertain – it's all I've done since I could

walk. I don't want more of the same.' Then with a soft-
ening of her voice and expression. 'Don't get me
wrong, Tazz. I have a fondness for Kip. I could easily
love him – or you, for that matter.'

'Me?'

She laughed. 'Don't sound so surprised. You're vice-
president of a bank, you're about as handsome as a
groomed stallion, and I'll bet you treat every woman
you meet like a lady . . . whether she deserves it or not.'

'The vice-president thing is only temporary. I took
the job with the understanding it would only be for
three months.' At her questioning look, he explained.
'It was an arrangement between Miss Hawthorn's father
and myself. He's the one who hired me.'

'Then what will you do?'

'I don't know.'

Ray uttered a sigh. 'Well, so much for our relationship.'

'You really should look for more in a man than a title
or his worth.'

'Yes, I know. Have some kids, work from daylight till
dark every day, and become an old woman by the time
I'm thirty. My mother only had one child, yet she died
from hard work when I was still a little girl.'

'I reckon following gold-strikes is about as hard a
road as anyone can travel.'

'In all my years, Tazz, I've never been on a real holi-
day. My father has ruled my life since the day I was
born.' A flush of anger came into her face. 'And I'm
tired of it. I want more out of life than to toil and slave
for the sake of customers. I want to experience some
fun and excitement. I don't mind working hard, but I

also want to frequent the theater and have nice clothes. I want to see a parade and visit the county fair. I want to have some enjoyment too.' She paused to take a breath. 'Is that being so greedy?'

Tazz smiled. 'Everyone wants something out of life. I expect your wants are no greater than most.'

She took the final bite of dessert from her plate and emitted a girlish giggle.

'One thing I want is another piece of pie – before it's all gone.'

'I'm afraid I've eaten all I can.'

'Will I see you tomorrow?'

'I'll probably attend the Sunday meeting and see what the day brings.'

She scraped up the last bit of dessert and forked it into her mouth.

'OK. Maybe I'll see you and maybe I won't.'

Tazz placed two silver dollars on the table, twice what was required to pay for his meal and both desserts. 'Thanks again for telling me about the fresh peaches.' He winked. 'It was almost as sweet as the company.'

Another giggle. 'The pleasure was mine, Mr Vice-President of the bank.'

Tazz picked up his hat and left the room. Colena purposely avoided looking in his direction. It had been no accident she had walked in to see Ray kissing him. He knew the young woman's idea had been for Partee to see the act. Somehow, he had gotten in the middle of Ray trying to make Partee jealous.

Yeah, and it backfired into having Colena think I'm chasing after ReAnn!

Once out into the dusk, he wandered past the bank

and took a check of the doors. The place was locked up tight. Furthermore, there was very little money in their vault to steal. The mason had the bricks on hand and was going to brick in the safe in the next day or two. Tazz would feel a lot better about the security of the bank once he knew no one could simply bust the door down and haul away the safe.

He considered what Ray had told him about Worthington. Despite the peach pie dessert, he had a bad taste in his mouth. Tazz could see the unfair conditions forced upon the miners and their families. The prices were inflated at the store and the deductions for the housing were about twice what they should be. Worthington was a giant leech, sucking the life blood out of the entire population of Penance. Colena's bank might help to change all that.

Thinking of her, his mind returned to her and Partee's being together. What was wrong here? He should have been the one having dinner with Colena, and Partee should have been sitting with Ray. How had everything gotten so backwards?

Get your mind off of that gal, he told himself. She's too good for you . . . and she darn well knows it!

CHAPTER NINE

Tazz walked down to check on his horse. After grooming the mare and spoiling her with a bag of oats, he visited some with the livery man. He left the stable, wandered along the main street and made a circle of several buildings. When he passed the smokehouse, which sat behind the company store, he noticed something amiss. There was no guard!

Hurrying over to the door, he found it locked. He paused to study the ground for a moment. No blood, no suspicious tracks. Everything looked OK . . . except for there being no guard at the smokehouse door.

'Mutt?' he called from his side, 'are you OK in there?'

He heard a muffled sound, but nothing he could understand. Tazz pulled his gun and carefully drew back the bolt lock. He pushed the door open, while he stayed far enough back to react to any kind of attack. However, Mutt was not inside. Boyle was there – gagged and bound, lying in the middle of the room!

Tazz quickly untied him and removed the cloth from his mouth.

'Blast it all!' Boyle swore and began to rub circulation back into his wrists. 'Somebody clouted me a good one.' He paused to gingerly finger a lump on the back of his head. 'I didn't see or hear nothing, then *whap*! I'm out cold and wake up lying on the dirt floor.'

'And Mutt is gone.'

'That's plain to see,' Boyle agreed. 'I'd have been bound up here till Peters came with breakfast if you hadn't come along.'

'How long ago this happened?'

'Maybe a couple hours,' Boyle answered. He tried to get up, but sank back down and held his head with both hands. 'I'm out of the chase for a bit, Spencer. My head feels like a split melon.'

'You take a few minutes to get feeling better. Then pass the word about the escape. I'll see if I can pick up Mutt's trail.'

'Who would help one of them rotten kidnappers?' Boyle wanted to know.

'I intend to find out.'

'Good luck, Spencer. Watch yourself.'

Tazz said 'so long' and hurried off to get his horse. He pondered the timing of the jailbreak. The circuit judge was due to arrive in a couple days. There would have been a quick trial and a sentence handed down. However, he had to wonder if the escape was prompted by the coming of the judge. Or was it more than a coincidence that Mutt should escape on the very eve of the day Worthington's money was due to arrive?

Colena sat on the porch of the boarding-house. She wanted to talk to Tazz and smooth things over between them. She felt rotten about telling him he was only a figurehead. Worse, she couldn't stop the gnawing in her stomach and ache in her heart at having seen him kissing another woman!

Millie spied her sitting outside and came out to join her.

'Are you hungry, dear?' she asked. 'I have some left-overs warming on the stove.'

'I've already eaten, Millie. Have you seen Mr Spencer?'

'I caught sight of him an hour or so back. He was coming down the main street from the stable. A few minutes later, I saw him return to the stable and leave with his horse. I guess he wanted to give his hay-burner some exercise.'

Colena frowned. Why would Tazz go for a ride after dark? Something didn't feel right. She bid a quick farewell to Millie and left the boarding-house. Tolken or Partee might know what was going on. One of them might be at the Open Pit saloon.

It was between hours for the establishment. The dining area was empty, while there were a few men on the bar side, and a couple gambling tables were busy. She didn't see Partee or Tolken.

'Yuh want something to eat?' A gruff voice practically demanded an answer.

She whirled to see ReAnn's father. A dark glower shone on his face. 'I came here early,' she said. 'Have you been reduced to waiting tables, Mr Gannon?'

He snorted with contempt. 'That worthless, good-for-nothing daughter of mine done skedaddled after the supper dishes were done. I'm thinking she run off with Partee.'

'Actually, I was looking for Mr Spencer. I see he isn't here.'

'I 'speck you won't see him either, not since the escape.'

'Escape?'

'The fellow in the smokehouse, the one called Mutt. Someone clubbed Boyle over the head and broke him out.'

'Aren't you afraid he might have grabbed your daughter? I mean, he and his friend kidnapped me!'

'He was already gone before Ray done sneaked off.' Then his face grew as cold and rigid as if it was chiseled out of ice. 'Tell you one thing – when I get my hands on that no-good girl of mine, I'll darn well teach her not to run away again. I'll beat her until she can't stand up!'

Colena winced inwardly, fearful the man meant every word. In fact, she was suddenly frightened even to talk to him.

'Thanks for your help,' she blurted quickly. 'If you should see Mr Spencer, would you tell him I'm looking for him.'

'Yeah, as if I ain't got enough to do.'

She didn't reply, but hurried out of the building. She had no trouble believing Mr Gannon was the sort to use cruel punishment on his child. Having seen the ominous look on his face, she feared, if ReAnn should return, he would severely injure the poor girl.

'There you are!' a voice called behind her.

Phil Tolken was on the walk. He displayed his usual smile. 'I missed you at the boarding-house. Spencer asked me to give you a message.'

'I've been searching all over town for him!'

'Yeah, he told me he thought the break from the smokehouse might be tied into the arrival of

Worthington's money. He rode out of town a couple hours ago.'

'And no one told me until now?'

'Not much anyone can do about it,' Phil said. 'We haven't got any law except for the regulators. One of them is in bed with a headache, while the other is asleep from being on guard for twelve hours.'

'Something is dreadfully wrong. This has to do with the money transfer coming in tomorrow, I'm sure of it!'

'Worthington's money is due here tomorrow morning?'

'That was the schedule.'

Phil grunted. 'Well, there you are. I'd say Spencer was right.'

'Did you see which direction he went?'

Phil arched his brows in surprise. 'You aren't thinking of following after him?'

'He might need help. If someone aided Mutt's escape from the smoke house, it means there are at least two men to deal with.'

'If I remember right, your vice-president killed four bandits in a single gunfight. Two men would hardly be a challenge for him.'

'Would you ride with me?' she asked Phil. 'I don't know the trails around here.'

The newsman scratched his head. 'I guess I could try and get a story out of this – a first-hand sort of thing.'

'Yes, that's the spirit!'

'Unless we find ourselves in the middle of a gun battle and shot full of holes.'

'No grit, no glory!'

'Nice motto.' He grinned. 'Perhaps we can have

those words engraved on our tombstones.'

'Will you go with me or not?'

He laughed and gave an affirmative nod. 'When do you want to leave?'

'At first light.'

'OK, Miss Hawthorn. We'll ride out and make a little destiny of our own.'

They agreed to meet before daylight and Colena returned to the boarding-house and went to bed. She knew she wouldn't sleep, unable to think of anything but finding Tazz. Phil was probably not much of a tracker, but he should know the route the courier would take coming from Denver. Oddly enough, her concern was not for the money, it was for the safety of Tazz!

It was mid-morning when Tazz spied the third set of hoof-prints. He had been following the tracks of only two animals. It appeared there had been some hesitation, then the horses had changed direction. After a few minutes, he located a man, well off the main trail, bound to a tree. His hat was gone and he had a gag in his mouth. A lesser tracker might have missed the sign. He stopped his mare and jumped down to untie the victim.

The man gasped, as soon as the gag was removed.

'Thank the Lord!' he exclaimed. 'I'm sure glad to see you, friend. I've been thinking of the hungry bears and mountain lions that might be searching these hills for food.'

'You're the courier, the one with Worthington's money. Are you hurt?'

SPENCER'S LAW

'Only my pride,' he said. 'They took me without a fight.'

'How many were there?'

'Two men. They wore bandannas over their faces. One of them was a sizable man. He did all of the talking. The other fellow was dressed in a black suit.'

'How long ago did this happen?'

'Maybe an hour.' He rubbed his tender wrists. 'They took the money and my horse. I had two bags of cash – five thousand in each. I heard a shot a short while back.' He grimaced. 'I think they killed my horse.'

'Probably as a safety measure, in case you worked yourself loose.' Tazz paused to search the ground with his eyes, then pointed. 'They headed off in that direction?'

'Towards the trail to Leadville,' the courier answered. 'I kept watch, but I didn't see or hear anyone circle back.'

Tazz gave the man a drink from his canteen.

'It's about ten miles into Penance. Think you can walk that far?'

'With no horse and afoot, I don't guess I have much choice.'

'I can't let the trail get cold, and this country is too rough for my mare to pack double.'

'No argument here,' he said. 'I'm just real glad you come by when you did. You get them jaspers for me.'

Watching the ground, Tazz picked up the tracks of the three horses. After a short way, he spotted the courier's animal, munching grass, as if without a care in the world.

Tazz had an idea of where the Leadville trail intersected. He continued to move at a rapid pace, until he spied a second saddled horse. Its reins were dragging and he was standing as if waiting for his rider.

Tazz took a sweep of the area with his eyes. After a short search, he located a dark form on the ground. It took only a moment to identify Mutt's sizable bulk. He swung over and gave the man a quick examination. He was dead. The gunshot the courier had heard had not been his horse, it had been Mutt being shot in the back. Rather than take time to catch up the horse and load the body, Tazz pushed ahead. The second bandit wouldn't be expecting the pursuit to be this close. He would probably take his time and ride easy, until he hit the main road.

Pushing his mount hard, Tazz made good time. He was about a hundred yards from the trail to Leadville, when he caught sight of two people standing together. He recognized Partee and Ray! They were both holding the reins to their horses and appeared to be in heated conversation.

He closed the distance to 200 feet before Partee saw him. The man spun about and yanked his pistol free. He fired once, but the bullet tore through the nearby branches. Tazz drew his own handgun, ducked low over the saddle and kicked his horse into a charging run. At such a pace, the animal stretched out, bearing down hard, cutting the space between them.

Partee lifted his arm and took careful aim. Before he could fire, Ray grabbed his arm. She wrestled with him for a moment, but he batted her away.

Tazz gauged the distance, closing to a decent range for a handgun. Partee was in a panic now. He fired twice more, but he was rushed and excited. Both bullets sang harmlessly over Tazz's head. In return, Tazz took a steady aim and fired one time.

Partee jerked backward, as the bullet dusted a tiny hole in his vest. Stunned, his eyes widened with shock and he lowered his gun until it was pointing at the ground. Tazz pulled his mount to a jarring halt, less than fifty feet away, ready to fire a second time. But Partee didn't try to shoot again.

'Drop the gun!' Tazz hollered the warning. 'Drop it now!'

Partee stared at him with glazed eyes, his face blank. Instead of dropping his weapon, his knees folded and he slumped onto the ground in a heap.

'No!' Ray cried, dropping down at the man's side.

While Tazz dismounted, Ray turned Partee over and lifted his shoulders, cradling his head in her lap. A red blotch had spread across the man's fancy vest. His eyes were still open, but he would never see again. Partee was dead.

'I had to shoot back,' Tazz said gently.

Ray's face was contorted in anguish. 'It's all my fault,' she lamented, sniffing at her tears. 'He did this for me.'

'What do you mean?'

'I made him jealous, so he would leave Penance and start over. I wanted him to take me away. I didn't know he intended to steal the bank's money.'

'I'm afraid he was also behind the kidnapping of Colena Hawthorn.'

Her head snapped up, aghast at the news. 'What? he was involved in that?'

'It all fits. He was the one who hired Mutt and Jigger.

151

He led the posse and was supposed to follow me. When I discovered the hide-out, they were waiting for me. I couldn't understand how they knew I was there.'

'Kip warned them?'

'He followed my trail long enough to know I was going to locate the cabin. Boyle and Peters said he left them for a couple hours, while he supposedly did some scouting on his own. He wasn't searching for my trail, he rode circle around me to warn his men.

'When I got the best of his boys and Mutt was captured, the man kept his mouth shut, confident Partee would get him out. He did that last night.'

'Mutt escaped?'

'I've been trailing them both since they left Penance. I figured the money being scheduled to arrive today was no coincidence.'

'My poor Kip.'

'Partee has been trying to get a pile of money any way he could. When the kidnapping attempt failed, he decided to grab the money Worthington was transferring to the bank.'

'He kept promising he had a plan to make a lot of money. He was going to take me away.' Ray's voice cracked. 'I didn't think he would turn to kidnapping or robbery.'

'Murder too,' Tazz informed her. 'He killed Mutt. I found his body back down the trail a piece.'

'Good Lord, Spencer!' She sniffed tearfully. 'It's all my fault!'

'A man makes his own choices,' Tazz told her gently, placing a consoling hand on Ray's shoulder. The girl flinched under his touch and he glimpsed the bruised flesh about her lower neck. He pulled the material back enough to see several dark abrasions.

'What happened?'

'Pa saw me kiss you,' she murmured. 'He wanted to teach me a lesson.'

Tazz gnashed his teeth, feeling as if a braid of barbed wire had been tightened around his chest. This woman had been servant and slave to her father for over twenty years. When she took a moment for romance, he beat her. Was it any wonder she was desperate to get away?

Ray lowered Partee's head to the ground and got stiffly to her feet. With a sorrowful expression, she heaved a sigh. 'I feel so dirty and ashamed, Tazz. I never did love Kip. I just wanted a way out.'

'He asked you to meet him here?'

'Claimed he had been saving scrip ever since Worthington hired him. With the bank ready to exchange money for the scrip, he said he was cashing it all in.' She grunted her disgust. 'It was all a lie. Worthington never allowed anyone an extra dime to live. That buzzard uses his wealth and power to control everyone in Penance.'

'He's a tyrant all right.'

'Tyrant is too nice a word,' Ray said angrily. 'You remember how I told you about when I went after him?'

'I believe you mentioned something about it.'

'Well, he wanted to . . .' she squirmed uncomfortably, 'to fully appreciate my wares. I said no – not until we were married.' She ducked her head in shame. 'He laughed at me, Tazz. He said he would never marry a trollop like me.' Tazz didn't have a response to her admission and Ray continued. 'He actually laughed,

Spencer.' Her voice became laced with bitterness and humiliation. 'He even spread the rumor that I had surrendered my virtue to him!' She lowered her head, suffering from the memory of her disgrace. 'Kip was about the only one who believed my side of the story.'

Bile rose up inside of Tazz.

'The filthy, rotten maggot.'

Tears once more filled her eyes. 'My father heard the gossip and took a strap to me.' She grimaced at the memory. 'Do you know what it's like? To be full-growed and have someone used a strap across your bare back?'

The words drove spikes into Tazz's conscience.

'I'm sorry, Ray, real sorry.'

She regained a measure of composure. 'I tried to win Worthington's heart and discovered he doesn't have one. Kip tried to make a dream come true and Worthington dashed his dream to bits.'

'The man deserves a through whupping,' Tazz said.

'And I'm destined to end up slaving at the Open Pit, spending my nights entertaining miners.' She sighed her resignation. 'Pa is going to beat me again and Worthington can sit back and laugh at my ignorance.'

Tazz made a decision and walked over to Partee's horse. There were the two pouches tied behind the saddle. He removed a bundle of money from one and transferred it to the saddlebags on Ray's mount. At her curious frown, he gave a tip of his head.

'If you stay on the main trail, you can reach Leadville in a couple hours. If it was me, I'd opt for a stage to the nearest rail station and head back East. A young lady, with a fair sum of money to support her, should be able to find a new life and a proper young gentleman to settle down with.'

Ray's expression was one of astonishment. 'Tazz! What are you saying?'

'I'm convinced you knew nothing about the robbery or kidnapping.'

'No! I didn't! I swear!'

'Well, I'm returning with the two robbers and the money – less your reward for saving my life and helping to prevent the theft.'

'I can't . . .' She was crying again. 'Oh, Tazz, you don't know . . .'

'Way I see it,' Tazz argued. 'Mr High-and-Mighty owes both you and Kip a fair share of money for his deeds. Maybe this will set the record straight.'

Ray was so choked up, she couldn't speak. She stepped forward and hugged Tazz for a few long seconds. Then she leaned back, blinked through glistening tears and stared up into his eyes.

'We could always share the money together?' she offered. 'I could wait for you in Leadville?'

He shook his head. 'I've got a lady waiting for me back in Penance.'

Ray glanced over his shoulder and stiffened. 'Ouch! I don't think she's in Penance just now.'

As Tazz turned to look at an approaching rider, Ray broke away and climbed stiffly up onto her horse. She paused to smile down at him from the perch.

'Knowing what a resourceful man you are, Tazz Spencer, I'm sure you can explain why you were holding me in your arms just now.'

Tazz stood numb, unable to move.

Colena came riding out of the woods as Ray dug her heels into her horse's ribs. As one animal raced away from where Tazz was standing, the other came rushing towards him at full tilt.

When Colena jerked her horse to a stop, Tazz quickly moved over to help her down. She cast a look in the direction of Ray, then her eyes settled on the body of Partee.

'I about kill myself getting here,' she panted, 'and I find you wrapped in the arms of another woman!'

'She was saying goodbye.'

'Tolken and the courier are behind me. They had to catch up Mutt's and the courier's horses. You saw Mutt had been killed?'

'Partee shot him in the back.'

'What about the money?'

'I managed to get most of it back.'

Colena's face darkened in a scowl. 'Most of it?'

'I reckon the bandits must have split the cash and hidden some of it somewhere along the trail. I doubt we'll ever find it.'

She gazed off in the direction Ray had ridden, obviously not buying his story.

'I don't suppose you had time to count how much was missing?'

'I'd guess about two thousand dollars.'

'Worthington is going to be furious.' She spoke the obvious.

'Yeah, well, I'm not all that concerned about what Worthington thinks. The guy is an unscrupulous, low-life maggot.'

She lifted her brows in surprise. 'Such harsh

language, Tazz. I might think you dislike the man!'

'What's to like?' Tazz asked. 'He's the kind of rich scum who uses women for his own entertainment, then casts them out like dirty laundry. He even tried to win my girl over with his fancy carriage, his big house and all his money. He can count himself lucky that I bothered to get any of his money back.'

'It was lucky for us too, Tazz. We'll need the rest of the currency to run our bank and be able to handle the scrip exchange.'

'*Our* bank?' he asked.

'I'm going to need a strong vice-president, Tazz,' she said softly. 'A man I can count on to always be at my side.'

He gave a little tug and Colena willingly came into his arms. 'I reckon things have a way of working out for the best.'

She smiled. 'I reckon they do at that.' Then she kissed him in a way that removed any doubt as to how things would work out!